TEXAS

1857

I0663768

Texas 1857: Birth of a Gunman
By Ronnie Ashmore

Published by Creative Texts Publishers, LLC
PO Box 50
Barto, PA 19504
www.creativetexts.com

ISBN: 978-1-64738-064-9

Birth of a Gunman

RONNIE ASHMORE

CONTENTS

1

The riders came from nowhere. At least it seemed that way to young Johnny Cole. To his nine-year-old way of thinking they just appeared out of the sky, like a butterfly or a mockingbird.

But these riders were not friendly like those things were. Johnny knew that by the way they rode their horses up into the yard, hard and fast. A sound like thunder filled the air from all the horses running into the yard at once. He also knew it by the way his mother grabbed his arm and rushed him into the house before the riders rode into the yard. She closed the door where he could not see out.

But Johnny was curious. He went to the front window, the place where the pane should have been was empty, as glass was hard to get way out here, or so his pa had said. He watched and listened to his mother talk to the rough men.

His mother was young, not even thirty yet, and very pretty. She was, Johnny knew, tough and not scared of anything. But she seemed scared now. Looking at the men, Johnny could almost feel his mother shaking from where he stood inside the house.

She looked the men over. The bearded leader and the dirty man next to him just stared at her, silently, the others looking around the small place.

"What do you want?" she asked, trying to keep her voice from shaking.

The men behind the two in front laughed. A quick glance back by the bearded man stopped the laughter.

He faced the woman, "Where's your husband?"

"Out. He will be back shortly."

"Out, huh?" the bearded one asked.

"He out tryin' to convince the neighbors that secesh isn't the answer to the problems this country is having?" the dirty man said.

"I know nothing of that, sir. Now, please leave," Johnny's mother said.

The dirty man looked at the bearded one and laughed. The others laughed with them.

"Sir and please. You a polite one, aren't you?" the dirty man said.

Wilma, that was Johnny's mother's name, backed up a step. Unsure what was going to happen. She wished she had grabbed the shotgun by the door as she shoved Johnny in the house. Now she stood with no gun and no chance of defense.

Johnny took a moment to look at the men, fear causing tears to form in his eyes. He wiped them away angrily. His pa had told him on numerous occasions that men did not cry, ever. Now it pained him to know he was on the verge of a full crying fit.

Wilma looked at the men. The dirty man took a rope from his saddle and shook a loop into it. He threw the rope over Wilma then backed his horse up, pulling her off the porch, into the yard. Her feet tangled; she fell to the hard ground.

She screamed a little scream that she stifled. She did not want to alarm Johnny. That was her only thought as the man dragged her toward the barn. Johnny must be kept safe.

From inside the house, Johnny watched as the men dragged his mother into the barn. He could hear her screaming, sounding as if she were in pain. He went to the front door and opened it slightly. Her screams seemed louder.

BIRTH OF A GUNMAN

He heard the men laughing as his mother cried out. Tears fell from Johnny's eyes. He could not stop them, no matter how hard he tried, he was failing at being a big boy.

If his pa were here his mother would not be crying and yelling, and the men wouldn't be laughing. He felt sure of that.

They were in the barn a long time, it seemed to Johnny, who stood fixed at the door peering out toward the barn. He heard one of the men laugh loud as he came out of the barn and say something about his mother being a fighter.

Johnny could not understand why they were fighting his mother, she never hurt no one in her life as far as he knew.

The bearded man stepped from the barn, putting his gun belt on, and adjusting his clothes.

The other men came from the barn then, all laughing and smiling. Johnny, for the first time counted the men. His pa would want to know how many had made his mother cry.

There were seven, no eight, one was still in the barn. Johnny heard the gun shot. It was loud enough to make him flinch and stare out at the barn through his tears.

The last man came from the barn, smiling, it was the dirty man. They mounted their horses and looked around the yard, back at the cabin. Johnny stood still.

The bearded man reined his horse around and left the yard. The others followed in his path. Soon they were gone, and Johnny was alone in the quietness of the cabin.

After a few minutes of searching for the courage to go to the barn, Johnny swallowed hard and stepped out onto the porch. His eyes fixed on the barn.

2

Johnny went into the barn slowly. As his eyes adjusted to the gloom he stopped in his tracks. He stared at the scene in front of him for a moment then ran forward and fell to his knees.

"Ma! Ma!" he said through tears and crying.

His mother lay on the barn floor in a pile of hay. Her clothes were gone, she was naked, and had bled from several cuts to her face and body.

Johnny realized that the reason she was not moving or answering him was because half of her head was missing. There was blood all over the barn floor, mixing with the dirt and hay. As Johnny looked around, he wondered if he could help fix his mother and she would be all right.

He was scared to try. He cried harder and buried his head in his hands. He backed away from the body that had been his mother. He leaned with his back to the barn wall and his knees bent to his chest. He cried.

Johnny was unsure when the neighbor from the place next to theirs came into the barn. But he was aware of being picked up by Mr. Goodson. When Johnny looked at Goodson as he was lifted from the barn floor he began to cry again and call out for his mother.

Goodson held the young boy tightly and said, "Hush boy. Your ma is gone. So is your pa."

Goodson carried Johnny out to the wagon he had driven over and placed Johnny in the back. There was a lump under a canvas tarp that Johnny sat down on, crying silently now. Not wanting to make Mr. Goodson mad.

Goodson came out of the barn carrying the lifeless body of Johnny's mother. He stood at the tailgate of the wagon and looked at Johnny.

"You gotta move, boy."

Johnny moved from where he was seated. Goodson, with Johnny's mother draped over one shoulder, took the free hand he had and moved the tarp from the lump Johnny had sat on.

As the tarp moved back, Johnny was shocked to see his father lying in the wagon bed. His neck twisted at an odd angle, his tongue, purple and swollen, sticking out of his mouth. As Johnny took in the sight of his dead father he began crying again, yelling for his pa.

Goodson dropped the body of Wilma Cole roughly into the bed of the wagon then looked at Johnny hard.

"Quit all that, boy. They are both dead and ain't comin' back no matter how much you squall."

Goodson climbed into the wagon and took up the reins. He looked back at Johnny, who was staring at the lifeless forms of his parents.

"We ought to bury them, I guess. We will plant them over on our place somewhere. The Secessionists will probably burn this place sooner or later."

Goodson popped the reins and the wagon jerked to a start. It slowly rolled away from the barn and the house that Johnny Cole had called home for all his life. The tears in his eyes had dried and now he just sat silent, staring at his dead parents. He couldn't shake the sight, his mother with half her head missing and his father with the odd twist to his neck.

He had heard the words Unionist and Secessionist before, but he did not understand what they meant. He doubted he ever would.

He climbed up to the front seat to sit beside Mr. Goodson. He looked at the man his pa had called a hard man. Johnny did not understand that phrase either. Today seemed to be a day of frustration and confusion, he thought.

"What do I do now, Mr. Goodson?"

The man looked at Johnny, "Well, no doubt you been dealt a rough hand, boy. We will make do. You can stay with me and ma until this whole war talk blows over."

Johnny was unsure what all he had said, but he did understand the part about staying with Mr. Goodson and his wife. Johnny liked Mrs. Goodson. She was always trying to make him laugh and smile when she saw him. That was before. Johnny was convinced he would never laugh again.

"Listen, boy. Don't let this change your opinion of your pa or ma. They did what they thought was right and that's that."

As they rolled along in the wagon, Johnny was feeling confused. He was unsure what an opinion was or why he should even have one in the first place. He looked back into the bed of the wagon at his parents.

All he knew was that at breakfast he had a ma and pa who loved him a lot, and now, before sunset he was alone in this world. He cried silent tears not wanting Mr. Goodson to know.

3

"Mitchell, are you daft? What are we to do with a nine-year-old boy?"

"We do with 'im what others do with their young 'uns. We raise him up and hope he does good in this life. Look, Martha, he ain't got no one else in this whole world. You want the county to take him? No tellin' what he'd become then."

They were standing on the porch talking in what they thought were hushed tones. Goodson earlier had buried Johnny's parents in a single grave at the edge of the property that used to be his home as Johnny had stood watching, crying silently. Now he waited on the wagon seat in the yard listening to what they were saying. To Johnny it seemed he wasn't wanted here either. He looked away pretending not to listen.

"Mitchell," Martha said in a longing voice.

"I'll hear no more about it. I won't have the boy runnin' feral."

Goodson stepped off the rickety porch of his cabin and walked to the wagon. He looked at Johnny and nodded with his head,

"Get on down boy. We will go get your clothes and stuff tomorrow."

Slowly, Johnny stepped down from the wagon and looked at the cabin that was his new home. It was not as nice as Johnny's house. That one had been painted and Pa was always fixing things around it.

This one looked to be ready to fall down. The porch was shaky, with missing boards. The wood was rotting in places and falling off in others.

It did not look like a safe place to Johnny. But then how safe was his other home. Maybe, Johnny thought, there were no safe places in all of Texas.

As Johnny climbed the stairs it all seemed strange to him. How was he going to ever be happy here at this place? He wanted to cry. But as Mr. Goodson had covered his Ma and Pa with dirt, Johnny vowed he would never cry again as long as he lived.

He went inside the cabin, following Mrs. Goodson. He looked at her and she smiled at him. He couldn't help but smile back.

"Johnny Cole. I swear I will give you a decent of a life as I can here in this God forsaken land that we call Texas," she scruffed his hair as she spoke to him.

Johnny looked at her a moment, then said,

"I don't want to be a bother, ma'am. I can go somewhere else."

"Nonsense. You are not a bother. Let me show you where you will sleep."

It was a two-room cabin, so there were not a lot of choices, Johnny thought as he followed her. At his other house he had his own room. Now, he saw he would be sleeping in the back of the main room on a pallet made on the floor. He stared at it, then looked questioningly at Mrs. Goodson.

"Temporary," she said as if she could read his mind. "We will add a room just for you as soon as we can."

Johnny only nodded. He sat on his new bed, which was a patchwork blanket laid out on the floor. He tried hard to remember his promise to never cry again. He looked up at Mrs. Goodson and smiled.

Mr. Goodson came into the house, room? Johnny was unsure how he should refer to the tiny cabin. The only door led outside. And the room was one large room that served as the kitchen and living room. There was only a small table in the center with chairs. Johnny figured that was where everyone would sit if company came over.

There were stairs that led to a loft on the far side of the cabin. Probably where the Goodson's slept, Johnny figured.

He was looking around the room or house or whatever he should call it when Mr. Goodson came over to him.

"Boy, we will get you settled and comfortable as we go. In the meantime, we have chores to do. I need you to help me. Can you pull your weight?"

Johnny looked up at him silent, confusion on his face. He stood to his feet and in the most adult voice he could muster, he said,

"I'll do what I can, sir."

Goodson smiled for the first time at Johnny. It made him feel better knowing that Mr. Goodson was a gruff and rough type of man but also, he could be nice.

"That's fine, boy. Come on."

"Mitchell," Martha said, stopping him in his tracks.

He turned to look at her.

"His name is Johnny, not boy."

Mr. Goodson looked at Johnny as if seeing him for the first time. He nodded his head.

"Fine. Come on, Johnny, let's work."

4

Weeks passed. Sometimes the days went fast, other times the days went so slow Johnny was unsure if the sun would ever go down.

There was a ton of work to do around the place and Johnny and Mr. Goodson did it all by themselves and alone. This gave Johnny time to know more about Mitch Goodson. And Johnny liked what he had known so far.

Goodson was a strong, fair, and honest man. He kept to himself and if he had any feelings about the war talk the grownups ventured in, he never let it show. Although he didn't understand the talk the adults made, he couldn't help but think that if his pa had kept his feelings hidden, his parents might still be alive.

They were working this evening in the lean to that served as a barn on the Goodson spread. The wood was missing on some parts of the roof but nevertheless, it was hot under it. Johnny was tying harness together the way Goodson had shown him a few days before. Mr. Goodson was sharpening an ax by hand with a whetstone. The stone made a scraping sound that was both bothersome and comforting at the same time to Johnny's ears.

Johnny looked over at Goodson, whose arms were constantly moving as he slid the whetstone over the ax head.

"Mr. Goodson? You know the name of the men who killed my daddy?"

BIRTH OF A GUNMAN

Goodson stopped sharpening the ax. He looked out from the lean to staring into the fields in front of him, silent for a long moment.

"I reckon I could guess. Why?"

"Will you tell me who they were? Especially, the one with the face scar."

Goodson looked at Johnny for a moment.

"Face scar? That sounds like Rick Palmer. Why you want to know?"

"I'm gonna kill 'im. And the others."

Goodson looked at Johnny. The boy's voice sounded so soft that for a moment Goodson was not sure he had heard correctly.

"You are, are you?"

Johnny nodded,

"May not be today. But when I get older and stronger, I plan on killin' the man."

"Killin' is a heavy thing, son. Might need to think on it a bit," Goodson said, setting the ax aside.

"Been thinkin' about it since that man took my ma to the barn."

Goodson turned and faced Johnny, his face streaked with sweat.

"Killin' is a heavy load. Most men can't bear up to it. You may change your mind later as you get older."

Johnny shrugged his shoulders, not knowing what to say. He never said much to anyone nowadays. He had to go to church with the Goodson's on Sundays and it always seemed that people would look at him with pity or sympathy in their eyes. Johnny hated that. He was starting to hate a lot of things easily now.

RONNIE ASHMORE

He walked to the edge of the lean to and looked off to the south where his house was. The men who killed his ma and pa, Secessionists Mr. Goodson called them, had not come back and burned the house. Not yet. It had only been less than a month.

Johnny felt a pulling in his heart to go back to his house. He needed to see if it was still there, to touch it once more.

He looked back at Goodson, who had picked up the ax and was sharpening it again. Johnny wished it were the Goodson's who had been killed and not his folks.

He instantly felt a twinge of guilt for such thoughts. The Goodson's had treated him nice. He at least had a roof over his head, though he didn't understand why he couldn't go to his house and stay.

Johnny slipped out of the lean to unnoticed by Mr. Goodson. He looked back toward the house to make sure he was not watched. He had no horse; the Goodson's only had a single mare they used for field work and pulling their wagon.

Undeterred, Johnny took off across the fields heading toward his house. He walked carefully to avoid making any more noise than necessary, but soon he found himself running. His legs pumping to carry him the two miles to the one spot he had thought of for weeks now.

He reached the edge of the property and glanced over where his parent's single grave lay, unmarked except for a rock Mr. Goodson had set upon the dirt mound.

Looking away, he started running again. He could see the house just ahead of him. He wanted to stay there forever.

5

Johnny stopped at the foot of the stairs leading to the porch. He was breathing hard, trying to catch his breath. His mind flashed to his mother standing on the porch defiantly talking to the men who would moments later kill her.

Johnny stepped up onto the porch slowly. He pushed the front door opened, looking for danger, and unsure if he would know it if he saw it.

The front door opened into a big sitting room. It was dark now and seemed lonely. Before, it had always seemed bright and loud.

To the right of the sitting room was the kitchen with the table and a big wood stove that served to prepare food and keep the house warm in the winter. It was cold now, ashes piled in the belly.

Slowly, Johnny wandered around the house, which seemed cavernous compared to the Goodson's house. He went on to look into the bedrooms. The one where his parents had slept, and then the room that had been his. Still was his, he thought.

They looked the same as the last time he had seen them. The beds made the way his ma liked; all his things were put away. He fought back tears. He had not cried since his promise to himself, he would not cry now.

He went into his parent's room. He was not allowed in the room when they were alive and now as he entered and looked around, he had a feeling of not belonging wash over him.

He made his way to the bed and looked at the places his parents had lain and slept. He touched the blanket. His hand brushed something hard, just under the big blanket on his ma's side of the bed.

He pulled the blanket back slowly. A gun. It was the pistol his father had kept around the house for his ma to use if needed.

Johnny reached out, touching it gently. He had shot with his father a few times, but not enough to know how to operate the complicated instrument. He lifted it by the handle as he had seen his father do.

It was heavy, not as light as his father had made it seem when he carried it around. Johnny struggled to raise his arm and hold the gun out straight. He couldn't do it. Even with both hands the gun tilted toward the floor in front of him instead of the wall where he wanted to aim.

"That gun is as big as you are, boy."

The voice scared Johnny, making him jump, causing him to drop the pistol on the floor. It landed with a thud. He stared at it a moment then looked to the bedroom door at the voice.

Mr. Goodson stood there watching Johnny. He nodded toward the pistol on the floor.

"Good way to blow your foot off," he said, stepping into the room.

He bent down and picked up the gun, looked at it, then down at Johnny.

"What are you doing? Why did you leave like that?"

Johnny was silent a short moment. He decided if he was going to be a man on his own, even at nine, he needed to start speaking his mind and standing straight.

BIRTH OF A GUNMAN

"I wanted to come home," he said.

"You don't like living with me and ma?" Goodson asked, placing the gun on the bed.

"You and Mrs. Goodson have been nice. But I want to be here."

Tears were burning Johnny's eyes. He fought to control himself. He did not want to cry. Ever again.

Goodson nodded, then sat down on the bed, looking at Johnny.

"I can understand that. But Johnny, the war is comin'. I don't know when, but it is comin'. This place will be lucky to be standing in three years. Hell, my place may be wiped out too. It's not safe to stay here. Especially alone."

Johnny was surprised. It was the first time he had heard Mr. Goodson speak that many words at once. Johnny did not know what he meant by war and stuff still standing, but he nodded as if he understood.

"Can you teach me to shoot?"

"So you can go after the men who killed your folks?"

Johnny nodded.

"You're nine years old, son. No. I won't do it."

Johnny looked at the gun on the bed, then at Goodson.

"OK. Then I'm staying here."

"You're making a mistake, Johnny. But I can't tell you what to do." Goodson stood, looking down at Johnny, "But if you don't come with me now, don't ever come to my place again. For anything. Ma has been good to you, but this is gonna cause her grief. I don't want to see you again. We clear?"

Johnny thought a long moment. A million thoughts racing through his young mind, he looked up at Goodson, who was watching him from the doorway, waiting for his answer.

"Thank you for everything, sir," Johnny stuck his right hand out in an offer of a handshake.

It was all Johnny could think to say at the time. Goodson looked at the small, offered hand. Turned and walked away.

6

After six days, Johnny was hungry. He was unsure how he would find any food to eat again. He sat on the porch and looked out into the dusty yard. His eyes drifted back to look at the barn. All he could see in his memory was his mother lying dead and battered on the dirty ground.

He shook his head to clear his thoughts. He considered, not for the first time since being alone, going back to the Goodson's. He always dismissed the notion as soon as he thought of it. They had no use for a child like him.

What kind of child was he? Johnny thought of that for a moment. His mind was not capable of following a thought path too far and soon he started thinking of other things. Like food.

He needed to get to town. If he could get to town, he could find someone to give a child a meal. He felt certain of that. But it was a long walk to town.

Too bad the horse his folks had owned was run off by the men who had invaded his life. He could have ridden that into town.

There were other horses though. The Goodson's had a horse they never hardly used much. Mr. Goodson had said the horse was too old to work anymore, but maybe Johnny could use him to ride to town.

Goodson would never let him borrow the old horse though. Johnny stood from his seat on the porch and rubbed his hand through his hair, the sweat making it cling to his scalp.

He would have to steal the horse. He thought a moment longer of that idea. He would take the horse into town, get some food, which he'd need to steal as well, then come back and return the horse. Could he do it?

He had never stolen anything in his short life. His father and mother had always been very strict on not taking anything that wasn't his. He was now thinking about, planning? on stealing not only a horse but also food from the stores in town.

Thinking about it would not get it done. And Johnny was hungry. He went into the house and stashed the pistol under his bed. He had taken to carrying the gun and practicing with it over the past couple of days. The gun was still too heavy for him to carry far.

He left the house heading on foot toward the Goodson place, cursing the heat as he went. The idea was seared into his mind, he would borrow the horse no matter what. He just could not get caught by Goodson.

The horse was in the corral like always. Johnny could see it from the place in the brush where he was hidden looking the place over.

The heat beat down terribly on Johnny's back as he squatted and watched the house. There was no movement or activity from the house.

Sneaking as quietly as he could, Johnny made his way to the backside of the barn. He kept the corral and horse between him and the house.

He could feel his heart pounding in his chest and his breathing was coming in gasps. He focused on quieting his breathing.

BIRTH OF A GUNMAN

He would not have time to saddle the horse. That thought hit him as he made his way into the barn door to grab the hackamore that was kept on a nail just inside the door.

Moving silently, hackamore in hand, to the pole gate of the corral, Johnny slipped the halter on the horse's head. He stroked the old horse and whispered to it as he had seen Goodson do.

He gently led the horse to the gate. Johnny pulled the poles that made up the gate. He dropped the heavy lumber as quietly as he could, but the two poles still thudded the ground. He looked toward the house; afraid the noise would give him away. Nothing. Johnny led the horse around the barn and back up the hill to where he had been hiding earlier.

Once in the safety of the hiding spot, Johnny could not believe his luck of having taken the horse undetected. He had heard the old people talk of Comanche stealing horses while the white men were sleeping. He wondered briefly if he had any Comanche in his blood.

Johnny led the horse slowly while he looked for something to use as a step stool to mount the horse. He found a rock and used it to climb upon the back of the tall, old horse.

He started walking the horse towards town. He could almost taste the warm food he would find from some kindly citizen that would have a soft spot for a child with no parents.

7

As Johnny approached town on Goodson's horse, his cheerful mood had turned foul. First, the horse walked slower than a snail's pace which convinced Johnny that he could have out walked the horse. Secondly, the old horse would just stop in the middle of the trail and blow for several minutes.

Luckily, Johnny had met no travelers on the trail and did not have to try to avoid anyone. Now, as he walked the horse slowly down the dirty main street of town, he looked for anyone that seemed to have a kindness to their look. Despite the fact people were going about their business, he found no one.

The horse stopped in the middle of the street and refused to walk any further. Johnny slid from the back of the horse and, with the hackamore rope in hand, tried to move the horse from the street to a hitching rail. The old horse refused to move. He flung its head in the air forcefully jerking the rope from Johnny's hand.

Johnny looked around for a moment. The few people out and about on the street seemed to pay no attention to him. Not knowing what else to do, he left the horse standing in the street.

He walked toward the restaurant that he could see from where he stood. He was reminded of his hunger as his stomach began to growl. He gently opened the door to the restaurant and peeked inside.

BIRTH OF A GUNMAN

It was empty, only a man and a big, heavy woman standing at the counter talking. Both looked his way as he stuck his head into the doorway.

Johnny pushed the door open and came inside. He figured he had gotten lucky finding no other people in the place. Then the big lady spoke.

"What can I do for you?" she said.

Her voice was loud and echoed in the emptiness. It caused Johnny to jump a little. Her hair was piled high on her head with a few strands hanging from the sides. He swallowed hard, trying to hide his nervousness.

"I'm hungry," Johnny said.

The lady looked Johnny up and down for a long time. He felt as if he looked a mess. He knew his hair was uncombed and in need of a cutting, his clothes were dirty and smelled of stale sweat, and his shoes were worn down and torn so his big toe showed from the left shoe.

She laughed, then said, "You don't look as if you have any money. Why would I feed ya?"

"I can work for a meal," Johnny said.

The man stood straight from where he had been leaning on the counter, he looked at the woman with a simple expression. Johnny waited for him to speak but he didn't. The woman was laughing again and shaking her head.

"I got this bum to help me clean up," she said, jerking a thumb at the man. "I don't need a helpless kid. Where did you come from anyways?"

Johnny decided he would answer no questions if he were not receiving any food. He stood there in silence.

"You don't talk much do you? Get on with yourself ragamuffin, I got no use for you here."

She moved from where she stood toward him as if to run him off. Then something caught her eye outside. Johnny watched as she squinted through the glass to the street then back to Johnny.

"Why is the law coming over here? Is he wanting you?"

Johnny looked to where the woman was looking. He saw the marshal heading his way. Panic set in on Johnny but there was nowhere he could run to. He stood where he was as the lawman came into the restaurant and looked at the three people.

"Mary? You know this kid?" he asked by introduction.

The woman called Mary shook her head, "He came in wanting food. I assume he had no money by the look of 'im."

"You're all heart, Mary. This is the Cole kid I believe. His family had a place south of here."

The marshal stood looking down at Johnny. Johnny was as scared as he had ever been, but he would not let the adults know this.

"The one whose pa was hung, and ma was kilt?" Mary said.

"The same one," the lawman said.

He looked at Johnny, "Thought you were staying with the Goodson's, but I guess not."

Johnny found the courage to speak, "Why do you guess that?"

"Goodson told me the other day you were alone at your old house. Now his horse is standing in the street. The one you rode into town. Goodson doesn't use that horse without something attached to it, like a wagon or plow or such. Besides, Goodson walked into town following you on the stolen horse. Let's go."

BIRTH OF A GUNMAN

Mary and the other man just stared at Johnny. The lawman led him outside toward the jail. Johnny could see Mr. Goodson standing out front watching him.

8

Goodson watched as Johnny was led into the Marshal's Office, he followed the lawman and his young prisoner inside. Unable to contain himself any longer, he grabbed Johnny by the shirt collar and spun him around.

"Boy? What in the world were you thinking? Why steal from me?"

Johnny stood silent, looking at the ground.

"He was at the restaurant trying to beg food," the marshal said.

Goodson looked at the marshal, "From Mary?" He looked back at Johnny, "I guarantee she didn't feel pity on you, you thieving bastard."

Johnny looked up at Goodson, "I'm not a bastard. I am just a…"

His voice broke and he quit talking, afraid he would start crying. That was the last thing he wanted to do, cry in front of Mr. Goodson.

The marshal spoke up, saving Johnny some embarrassment.

"We can lock him up and see if the judge will hang him next month for stealing your horse or…"

Goodson looked at the marshal the same time Johnny did. Hang! For stealing an old nag of a horse.

"Hang 'im?" Goodson said. "I don't want that. At all. What else?"

BIRTH OF A GUNMAN

"Well, he is an orphan by rights. We all know that. I can see if Miss Tucker will take him in at her place. She does that now and then, takes in the wayward child."

The marshal sat down in his chair at his desk. Goodson nodded as he looked at Johnny.

"That might be a good idea."

He dug in his pocket for money but did not have any to give. He smiled embarrassingly at Johnny.

"I was going to buy you a meal, boy. But I.."

This time the lawman saved Goodson the embarrassment of saying it out loud.

"No worries on that, Mitch. I'll buy the boy lunch then take him to Miss Tucker."

Goodson grinned at the marshal, looked at Johnny, and nodded. He left the office without another word.

Johnny looked to the lawman and was surprised to see the scowl on his face as he stared across the desk at him.

"I think you are an incorrigible little mess, myself. But if I hang a nine-year-old, I reckon there'd be no end to hanging kids."

Johnny wasn't sure if he should say something or not. He chose to stay silent, watching the lawman. The marshal was old, Johnny did not know how old, but his hair was starting to change colors on the side of his head.

The marshal stood, "You aren't gonna make me regret I didn't hang you, are you?"

"No sir, I don't think so anyway," Johnny said, uncertain of the tone the man was using.

The marshal laughed, a loud booming laugh that made Johnny jump from surprise. He followed the lawman out of the office into

25

the street. Goodson and his horse were nowhere in sight. The lawman and Johnny walked back to the same restaurant, the one with the mean lady, Mary.

Mary looked at them as they came in. She looked at the lawman then to Johnny.

"Thought he was a thief?" Mary said.

"Nope. This is Johnny Cole. And Johnny Cole is one of the good guys." He looked at Johnny, "Right, Johnny?"

Johnny nodded his head grinning at the lawman.

"Jesus, Burt. You'd take in any stray that came along; I think. What will you have?"

They placed their orders and waited. Johnny felt better than he had since his parents had been killed. He knew the marshal would eventually ask questions; Johnny knew he would answer the lawman as honest as he could. He liked the man.

"Why are you not stayin' with the Goodson's anymore? They seem like nice people."

Johnny looked at the marshal for a moment, then shrugged his shoulders.

"Seems they didn't need me under foot causin' more trouble. They barely got enough for themselves."

"How long were you at your old place?"

Another shrug, "Few days. I was hungry. That's why I took the horse. I didn't know Mr. Goodson would get angry."

The marshal sat quiet, he just stared at Johnny, making him feel uncomfortable as the look continued. Finally, the marshal leaned in toward Johnny and looked into his eyes.

BIRTH OF A GUNMAN

"You're lying to me, boy," he said quietly. "If you thought you were in the right, you'd have asked permission instead of just taking what isn't yours."

Johnny had no answer. He let the lawman's words settle into his mind.

9

After they had eaten their meal, they then headed to a house that stood at the edge of town. The town was divided into sections. The businesses were all along the main street with the saloon and livery at one end of the street and the church at the other. The houses were built just behind the main street along the side roads. It was on one of these roads they walked along silently after leaving the restaurant.

They came to a house that looked like it needed to be torn down. Its porch was leaning to the left so awkwardly Johnny was sure it would fall if they stepped up on it.

The boards were sun baked and whitewashed from too many Texas summers. Johnny eyed the house suspiciously, then looked up at the marshal, who was watching Johnny.

"I know. It don't look like much. But Miss Tucker is a good lady and well thought of in this town. If you steal from her, I will hang you," he smiled as he looked at Johnny.

"I don't want to steal no more, sir. My pa and ma would be ashamed of what I did if they were here."

"That's good. Always remember that."

He nudged Johnny forward and they crossed the yard and stepped up onto the porch. It didn't fall in as Johnny had feared. The door opened before the marshal knocked on it. A woman that instantly reminded Johnny of his mother stood in the doorway looking at both visitors.

BIRTH OF A GUNMAN

"Marshal Teague. What brings you by?" she said, looking at Johnny as she spoke.

"Miss Tucker," he said as he removed his hat. "This is Johnny Cole. I am wondering if you have room for a boy with nowhere to go."

She stared at Johnny for a moment, then smiled, and stepped back from the doorway to allow them inside the house.

"Of course. Come in."

The inside of the house was in better condition than the outside. The furniture in the main room was comfortable and looked new. The tables that were scattered throughout, Johnny didn't know what you called them, seemed well cared for. The house was clean and tidy.

There was a staircase that led upstairs on the left as he entered the main room. He cast a quick glance up the stairs, seeing nothing.

"How many children do you have here now?" Teague asked.

"Three. The poor things need someone. Two of their fathers went off to try to recruit for this awful talk of war folks have been making."

She offered them a seat on a comfortable couch. Johnny sat down, unsure if his dirty clothes wouldn't stain the couch beyond future use.

She sat in a chair across from them and looked at Johnny a moment, then said,

"What happened to your folks, Johnny?"

Johnny stared at his worn-out shoes, feeling more out of place here than at the Goodson's. He summoned the inner courage to answer this nice lady's question. He looked her in the eyes.

"They were killed. I don't know by who. Or even why."

"You poor thing. Too much of that is going on around here, Marshal," she said, looking at Teague.

"Ma'am, war talk is all the talk there is nowadays. The men are dead set on having their voices heard. But still, this young man's folks were killed in a hard way."

She stood suddenly, without preamble, and looked down at the lawman.

"Very well. He is here now. I will care for him as long as he will listen and follow my few rules."

Johnny stood too, looking up at the kind woman.

"I will ma'am. I will do my best."

Teague stood up and walked to the door. He looked back at Johnny and Miss Tucker. He smiled at the lady, then looked at Johnny.

"Johnny, if you want to earn some money, not much mind you, but some. Come down to my office and I'll find something for you to do."

He left, closing the door behind him. Johnny stared up at Miss Tucker, who was looking down at him.

"First thing is a bath," she said, as she led him to the kitchen area just on the other side of the room they were in.

A bath! Johnny was already having doubts about his stay.

10

The next day Johnny was up early before the sun was up. He could already hear Miss Tucker in the kitchen cooking breakfast. The smells of the food cooking caused his stomach to make noises.

He looked around his small room. It was tidy, with a small dresser and a nightstand. The dresser was empty. He had no clothes to put in it.

He would meet the other kids that stayed here this morning. He was dreading that because the clothes he had were worn and threadbare. He felt certain that the others would make fun of him. He vowed he would not show it if it upset him.

He rolled out of bed and dressed quickly then made his way downstairs to visit with Miss Tucker.

She was in the kitchen making biscuits as he came into the room. She glanced at him a moment, going back to her task at hand.

"You're up early, Johnny Cole," she said, placing bacon in a pan to fry.

"Yes, ma'am. I ain't much on sleeping late, I guess."

She looked at him.

"Ain't? Is that the proper word?"

Johnny shrugged.

"I don't reckon I know the proper word, ma'am."

Miss Tucker went back to fixing breakfast and said nothing else. Johnny stood awkwardly in the kitchen a moment, then drifted to the main room.

He sat on the couch and looked at the room that was lit only by two lamps that sat on opposite sides of the large room. The gloom was heavy, and Johnny felt himself getting sleepy.

Miss Tucker came into the room wiping her hands on a towel. Her dark hair was pulled back in a severe bun, her apron was covered in dough and wet in places. She looked at Johnny as she wiped her hands.

"You want something to drink?"

"I ain't had coffee in a long spell," he said looking at her.

She finished wiping her hands and held the towel in front of her.

"It will be a spell longer too," she said, tossing the towel playfully at Johnny, who caught it and instantly laughed.

"And stop saying 'ain't'."

She grabbed the towel and headed back to the kitchen. In a moment she returned holding an empty pail.

"Will you go fetch water from the creek out behind the house here?"

Without a word Johnny took the pail and went outside. It was dark still, with only a hint of daybreak to the east. The trail was a well-worn path that could just be seen in the darkness. Johnny walked slowly down to the creek.

He was walking back with a full bucket of water trying to take care not to slosh it everywhere.

"Are you old lady Tucker's latest stray?"

The voice came from beside the house startling Johnny, almost causing him to drop the bucket. He looked in the direction the voice had come from, too scared to speak.

BIRTH OF A GUNMAN

"Figures you are. Well, some of us have been here a long time with her and her stupid rules. You ain't no different than anyone else who comes through here."

Johnny looked closer at the place where the voice came from. He could just make out a person standing in the shadows though it was still too dark to see the person clearly.

The shadow moved and disappeared to the front of the house leaving Johnny alone. He carried the bucket of water into the house and sat it down in the kitchen where Miss Tucker could get to it.

"That took a while. Everything all right?" she asked as she watched Johnny sit the bucket down.

He looked up at her, he grinned a shy grin.

"My first trip. Tomorrow will be better."

She laughed a soft laugh then went back to her work. For a moment, Johnny felt as safe and comfortable in the kitchen with Miss Tucker as he ever had in his own house with his mother. That feeling scared him a little.

11

They sat down to eat breakfast about a half hour later. Johnny took a seat at the end of the table looking at the food that was piled high on the table in front of him. Miss Tucker watched him with a grin on her face. Johnny heard footsteps coming down the stairs, loudly.

He turned to look in the direction they came from. The first person through the door into the kitchen was a tall boy who seemed older than Johnny's nine years and was bigger than Johnny was as well.

He was followed by two other boys who were not as tall or big. They all looked at Johnny as they sat down. The bigger one was the one that spoke.

"You're in my chair," he said, standing beside Johnny and looking down at him.

Johnny recognized the voice as that of the person that stood in the shadows earlier and scared him while he was carrying water.

The other two boys did not look up, but cast sideways glances at each other, giggling softly.

Johnny thought to himself as he looked up at the bigger boy, this was a test and whether he passed or failed, it would determine how his time in the Tucker house would be spent. Johnny summoned all the courage he had as he answered the boy.

"Not today. Today it's mine."

"What did you say?" the boy asked.

BIRTH OF A GUNMAN

The other two boys stopped giggling and looked at Johnny full on and wide eyed.

Johnny motioned his head to an empty chair.

"Food is getting cold."

Miss Tucker looked at the boys for a moment, then said,

"Oh, Phillip, sit down please. Let's eat before the food is cold."

Phillip looked at Miss Tucker then back at Johnny. He grabbed a biscuit from the platter and turned to Miss Tucker.

"I don't want to eat your slop lady."

He stormed out leaving Miss Tucker looking after him. Johnny wasn't sure, but he thought he saw tears glimmering in the corner of her eyes. She had worked on the breakfast for a long time this morning. He felt instantly sad for Miss Tucker and hot hatred for Phillip.

She looked at the three boys sitting at the table and smiled.

"Let's eat boys."

She spooned piles of scrambled eggs and biscuits onto each of their plates and made introductions as she did so.

"Johnny, this is Vernon and Chad. The one that just left is Phillip, he's the oldest here."

Johnny nodded to the other two, not forgetting how they were giggling while they thought Phillip had the upper hand.

After breakfast and the cleanup, the boys were free to go about their day. The other two, Vernon and Chad, went off to school.

Hearing Miss Tucker talk of school made Johnny nervous so he disappeared from the house as quietly as he could. Johnny had never been in a school before. His mother had taught him to read a little and write some. Mostly his name was the extent of what he had learned.

Still, he had no desire to go to a school where boys he did not like would be. Instead, he went out and, in the early morning light of the beginning day, made his way to the marshal's office.

The street was muddy, and the smell of manure and urine assaulted his senses as he went along. He carefully watched his step as he walked.

The office was locked and dark when he got to it. The lawman was nowhere in sight. Deciding he didn't have anywhere else to be now, Johnny continued to walk and explore the town.

He had been in town only a few times before, and always with his folks, usually taking care of getting supplies for the house and farm on a weekday.

The town seemed much bigger than he remembered. He tried in vain to recall what the town called itself. He couldn't remember the name. He made a mental note to find out the name of the town.

He turned the corner of a building and was in a long alley. He walked the alley careful to not step in anything like the trash and debris that lay scattered on the ground.

He turned the corner at the end going behind the businesses and came face to face with a big man that was as dark as the night.

It took Johnny a moment to catch his breath and regain his senses to stop himself from staring at the dark man, who stood watching him.

12

The man looked at Johnny, a scowl on his dark face.

"You evah seed a nigg'r 'fore, boy?"

"A what?" Johnny asked quietly.

"A darkie, a nigger. Tell me you nevah see one befo'," he said, stepping closer to Johnny.

Johnny shook his head,

"I never seen a man as dark like you. What happened to you? Too much sun? Does it hurt?" Johnny asked, stepping back a little.

The man stopped and stared at Johnny then laughed a loud laugh.

"Sun? Hurt? You a funny white kid," he said.

He looked around the area where they were standing then looked back at Johnny.

"Yous best be on you way. I get seen talkin' to you I might get hung up from a tree. That lawman is might particl'r abouts what we can do."

Johnny didn't understand everything the man was saying, but he understood enough to know the man was scared of being seen talking to him. Though Johnny did not understand why the marshal would care.

He looked at the black man a moment, then said,

"I'm Johnny Cole. What's your name?"

"Name? I don't know what my name is original, Johnny Cole. Folk 'round here call me Nigger Tom, though I s'pect that ain't what my family called me."

He looked at Johnny a moment longer.

"You ain't scared of me?"

Johnny shook his head,

"No. Should I be? I don't have any friends."

The man laughed again, louder this time, and slapped his leg with a big hand.

"Friend, you say! That's funny. I ain't no white man friend. I ain't your friend either. Now get on away from me before you get me kilt," he said, stepping back.

"Killed? Why would they kill you?" Johnny asked, not wanting the man to leave yet.

" 'Cause. I am a nigger talking to a white boy. Don't think you are immune either, folk around here kill whites who get friendly to the niggers too."

The man started to walk away. Johnny took a few steps closer to the big man.

"I'll be your friend, Mr. Tom," Johnny said.

The black man stopped and turned to face Johnny. He looked down at the boy a long moment, then said,

"No white man evah called me 'mister', boy. Why you do that?"

Johnny shrugged his shoulders.

"My folks taught me to call anyone older than me that. My folks are dead now, but I remember the rules they told me."

"Where you stay, boy?"

"Miss Tucker's. You know her?"

Tom smiled, nodded.

"Yeah, Miss Tucker a good woman. Probably the best woman for a white woman this town gots."

Johnny stood silent, not knowing what to say. Tom looked at him, and then smiled again.

"OK, Johnny Cole. I will be your friend. Though if I was you, I'd not tell nobody about it," he laughed a short laugh, then said, "I got to go, see ya 'round."

Johnny turned on his heels and ran down the alley back to the main street. He felt good inside. He had made his first friend in town. Though he did not understand why he couldn't tell anyone, it didn't matter. Tom would be his friend.

Johnny ran back to the marshal's office hoping the lawman would be there. Johnny liked Marshal Teague, though if asked he could not say why. He liked the way the man exuded calmness in talking with people.

Johnny was in the middle of the dirty street when a horse and rider nearly knocked him down. Johnny was unsure whose fault it was, but the rider reined in hard and glared down at Johnny.

"Watch where you're goin', you little bastard," the man said.

Johnny's reply, if any, was lost at that moment. He recognized the dirty rider who looked as if he needed a bath and shave in the worst way. Johnny was staring at the man openly, wide eyed.

The rider misread the look on the kid's face as fear of nearly being run over.

It wasn't fear Johnny felt. Johnny recognized the man from that day at the ranch. This was the man that had thrown the rope over his mother and dragged her off the porch.

RONNIE ASHMORE

The man spurred his horse and rode on. Johnny stood in the street watching him ride away. The man never looked back.

13

Marshal Teague was in his office putting the coffee pot on the stove to make when Johnny burst through the door. He was out of breath and was gasping to catch his breath so he could speak.

Teague looked at the kid, then shook his head.

"You run everywhere you go, you gonna wear yourself out, boy."

"I saw one of the men who killed ma," Johnny said, his breath coming in gasps.

"Saw? Where?" Teague turned to face the boy full on and looked down at him.

Johnny jerked a thumb toward outside,

"In the street. He was heading toward the livery just now."

Teague looked to the door of the office as if he could see through it. He looked back at Johnny.

"Describe him."

As Johnny gave the best description he could, Teague wrapped his gun belt around his waist. When Johnny was through talking, Teague said,

"You stay here. I'll be right back."

Johnny stood for a moment after the lawman left, then, tired of standing, he sat in the straight back chair in front of the marshal's desk.

After what seemed like hours but was only a few minutes, the marshal came back into the office and looked at Johnny.

"You sure that is the man you saw at your place that day?" he asked, sitting in his chair at the desk.

Johnny nodded.

"Why?" he said.

"That is Billy Snyder, that's why. Dirty Bill Snyder they call 'im. He is a scoundrel of a man."

"You gonna arrest him?"

"What for?"

"Killin' my ma," Johnny said, hating the pleading sound his voice had taken on.

"No, I ain't gonna arrest him. What happened to your ma was out of my jurisdiction, which is only here in town."

"But I saw him and his friends do it."

Tears were beginning to form in Johnny's eyes. He fought them back, determined not to cry.

Teague saw the tears forming and felt a little sorry for the young child who witnessed such brutality. But life on the frontier was full of brutality and young Johnny Cole was not immune to seeing it.

"Yeah, Billy probably did kill and rape your ma. He was probably part of the group that hung your pa too. Billy and his ilk have been making talk of how great it would be for Texas to secede from the union. War talk. That is what is on everyone's mind nowadays."

Johnny didn't understand half of what the lawman was talking about. War and secede. He had no concept of either thing.

But he did know that Billy Snyder had killed his ma. And now Teague was saying that Snyder had killed his pa. Johnny pound his hand on the desk, looking at Teague.

"I will kill him. I can do it."

Teague looked at Johnny a moment, then laughed a short laugh.

"Yeah, you could. I'd give it a few years though. Grow a little. Think about it."

"He will get away if something isn't done."

"Men like Snyder and his kind,

they never go away."

Teague stood and walked to the window, looking out into the street.

"Billy Snyder will be around when you get old enough to decide if killin' is what you want to do with your life."

"It's been decided. Since I found ma dead in the barn. I'm gonna get older and stronger and I will kill all the men who brought this down on my family. Bill Snyder, Rick Palmer, and any others I can find."

Teague turned to look at Johnny. The tone of the boy's voice froze him for a moment. There was a look on his face that Teague had never seen before on a boy.

He simply nodded, turned, and looked out the window again.

14

Johnny left the marshal's office. He had no place to go right now, and he felt like he didn't belong anywhere, so he went back to Miss Tucker's place.

As he entered the front door of the house that was for the time being his new home, he heard noises from the sitting room area. He entered the room slowly.

Sitting on a chair, a handkerchief held tightly in her hands, Miss Tucker had her head lowered. Johnny could see she was crying, and he instantly wanted to know why, and help her not cry anymore.

Johnny cleared his throat as he stepped closer to Miss Tucker's chair. She looked up, her eyes tear filled, surprised to see someone else in the room.

Johnny stood still, looking at her for a moment.

"Ma'am, what's wrong?"

Miss Tucker stood, wiped her eyes, looked at Johnny and smiled.

"Boys can be a handful sometimes, Johnny. Why are you back here? The others are at school, I think."

"I was at Marshal Teague's office," he said, not wanting to mention meeting Tom, his new friend.

"Well, we may have to get you into school. Let me grab my things and I'll take you there."

"Ma'am, can we do the school tomorrow, please?"

BIRTH OF A GUNMAN

She turned and looked at Johnny.

"Any reason we can't do it now?"

Johnny shrugged, saying nothing.

"What do you intend to do?"

"I want to go to my old home. Get some things, but it's a long walk from here."

"You want someone to go with you?"

"I can go alone, I just need a horse that I didn't steal."

Miss Tucker laughed a short laugh.

"Very well. I will take you to the livery and make arrangements. Is that OK?"

"All right," Johnny said.

He still wanted to know why she was crying. Although he felt sure it was because of the older boy, Phillip. Johnny had a bad sense being around the older boy and wondered how the other two got along with him. Time would tell.

Johnny went with Miss Tucker to the livery and was soon on a horse heading for his old home. As he rode, he glanced in the direction of the Goodson place. He could not see it from here, but he imagined Mr. Goodson was out working in the barn as he always was.

A slight pain hit Johnny as he thought of taking the old horse from the Goodson's. He vowed to himself he would never steal anything else.

The old house was still as Johnny had left it a few days ago. He dismounted and went inside to gather what clothes he could.

He found the pistol, with the sack that contained the ammunition. His clothes gathering forgotten, he carried the gun and sack out the back door.

RONNIE ASHMORE

The gun was heavy in his hands. He clumsily loaded the gun. Between dropping the percussion caps, spilling powder, and not being sure exactly how to load the heavy gun, it was a labor-intensive ordeal to get the six shots loaded.

When he was done loading, Johnny picked a target out. A tree was standing about twenty feet from where he stood just off the back porch. Using both hands to pull the hammer back, he lifted the heavy, long barreled gun and tried to aim.

The first shot went wild. Johnny wasn't sure where it landed because between the recoil, the explosion of powder, and the white cloud of gun smoke he could not see anything.

He lowered the gun and placed it on the ground. He shook his right hand to get the feeling back. He lifted the gun again and fired once more.

This time he saw where he hit. He had missed the tree by at least four feet to the right. He nearly choked on the smoke from the gun. The smoke was thick and hung in the air as there was no breeze to move it away.

He fired again. And again. He practiced the rest of the day shooting up all the balls that were in the sack. By the time he left with his clothes and the gun hidden safely in the bundle he carried, his arm ached, his hands were sore, and his ears were ringing to the point he could hear nothing. As he rode, Johnny was trying to remember if he had ever had so much fun.

15

The next morning Miss Tucker walked Johnny to the schoolhouse. It was literally a house, Johnny saw. The teacher was a man of about forty years old who looked at Miss Tucker as if she were the only woman he had ever seen.

Johnny felt uncomfortable being around so many other children. He saw Vernon and Chad sitting together in the back of the room and instantly decided to sit in the front of the class away from them. There was no sign of Phillip.

As the teacher, Miss Tucker had said earlier his name was Mr. James, continued to talk to Miss Tucker, Johnny tried to find a seat that was open. There were none open in front of the class. He took a reluctant seat next to Chad, saying nothing to the two boys.

Chad leaned over toward Johnny and said,

"You're gonna love it here. Nobody cares if you stay or leave."

Johnny nodded, not knowing what the boy was talking about. After a lingering silence, Johnny asked a question he had been holding in since he had seen Miss Tucker crying the day before.

"Where is Phillip?"

Vernon leaned in closer toward the two boys and smiled.

"He ain't here. May not be here today. Never can tell about Phillip."

Chad and Vernon laughed a little. Johnny looked at them both.

"Miss Tucker was crying yesterday. Do you know why?"

Chad looked at Vernon and they both laughed a little. Vernon put his hand over his mouth to keep the laughter stifled.

"Phillip told old lady Tucker that we weren't her kids, and we would do what we wanted," Chad said.

"She ain't our mother though she thinks she is," Vernon said, nodding toward Chad.

Johnny said nothing. He was remembering the gun he had tucked away in his belongings. He had smuggled the gun to his room in his clothes bundle, then found a hiding spot for the weapon.

Johnny did not like Phillip much, not since his first meeting with the boy. If he was treating Miss Tucker badly then maybe Phillip was no different than the men who had killed his folks. It was something to study on, that was for sure.

Miss Tucker finally left the small schoolhouse and Mr. James seemed different afterwards. He let the children go outside and play because he seemed to have lost focus on the studies.

Outside, the boys all played with the other boys and the girls played with the other girls. Johnny stood off by himself not playing with anyone. He did not feel he belonged at this place called school.

His mother had taught him studies at the house, teaching him to read and write along with some numbers. Now, he felt he would never learn more than what he knew now.

Johnny was leaning against the building in the shade watching the other kids. A whisper from behind the building caught his attention. He turned to see who was whispering.

It was Chad. He was at the rear of the building, peeking around the corner toward Johnny. He waved his hand fast, motioning for Johnny to come toward him.

BIRTH OF A GUNMAN

As Johnny rounded the corner behind the schoolhouse, he saw Vernon. He was standing with his hands in his pockets watching Chad. Then Johnny saw Phillip.

He was leaning against the wall watching both boys. He pushed himself off the wall when he noticed Johnny had seen him. He was sneering at him. Vernon and Chad switched positions to stand behind Johnny, blocking his retreat. Phillip stood in front of him blocking that way. Johnny could feel his heart beating faster as fear took over.

"Well, if it isn't Johnny Cole. Remind me again where do I sit during breakfast?" Phillip said.

It was a stupid thing to say. That was Johnny's first thought as he tried to form an answer. Nothing came to him except to look at Phillip straight on.

"If you forget, I'll remind you in the morning."

Vernon and Chad laughed quietly from their place behind Johnny. Phillip just glared at him, taking a step closer.

Johnny started to say something else, but the words never formed. Phillip hit him, hard, solidly in the mouth. Then Johnny was under attack by punches and kicks he never saw coming. He could hear the other two boys laughing as Phillip continued to beat on him. Johnny thought, as he was being hit repeatedly, that he was going to die

16

Johnny came awake slowly. It hurt to move his head too much. He lay there thinking about what had happened. He remembered Phillip hitting him and the other two, Chad and Vernon, laughing and encouraging Phillip to keep hitting him.

He tried to open his eyes, only one came open, barely able to focus. He saw someone sitting beside his bed. Johnny could not tell who it was. He tried to lift his head, which caused him to moan in pain. The figure beside the bed raised their head and looked at Johnny, standing to ease him back down on the bed.

Johnny stared with one eye at Miss Tucker.

"Ma'am? What are you doin' here?"

"You've been beat up pretty badly, Johnny. How do you feel?"

"Like I have been beat up." Johnny looked at Miss Tucker and tried smiling. "Am I blind?" he asked in a panic.

"No. At least I don't think so, but your eye is swollen, something fierce."

She smiled at him and somehow, he felt better, though he still hurt.

"Do you know who did this to you?"

Johnny ignored her question; instead he asked one of his own.

"How'd I get here? We were behind the schoolhouse."

"It was just you behind the schoolhouse when you were found. A local darkie found you, said he knew you stayed with me. I don't know how he knew that."

BIRTH OF A GUNMAN

Instantly, Johnny knew who she was talking about. His new friend, Tom. So, Tom had found him alone behind the school. The other boys must have left him. But what of the other school kids and the teacher, Mr. James? Johnny was silent for a long moment, lost in his thoughts until Miss Tucker's voice broke into them.

"That man scared me when he brought you to my door. But he said you were hurt and needed help. I guess that nigger saved your life, huh Johnny?"

Johnny looked at Miss Tucker a long moment, then said,

"Ma'am, I'd appreciate it if you would not call Tom and his kind nigger, please. Tom is my friend."

"Well, I wouldn't be bragging about that around town. It would get him and you in trouble most likely," she said.

Johnny said nothing.

"Who did this to you?"

"It's enough that I know and one day I'll settle it."

Johnny turned away from Miss Tucker and faced the wall not wanting to answer any more questions. Miss Tucker did not force the issue for which Johnny was glad. She left the room allowing him to sleep.

When he next awakened, it was Marshal Teague who stood over his bed looking down at him. Johnny looked up at the lawman and jumped with a start from surprise at seeing him there.

"Marshal."

"Young man, Miss Tucker says you won't say who beat you up. Why not?"

"It's not a big deal. I'll handle it later when I'm bigger."

Teague made a noise in his throat and shook his head.

"Another name for your killing idea, is that it?"

Johnny looked at him, nodded.

"Yeah. When the time is right."

Teague rubbed his hands through his hair and sat down in the chair by the bed.

"You sure do want to kill awful bad, don't you?"

"I don't want to, Marshal. I have to."

"Is that a fact?"

Johnny said nothing, just looked up at the lawman.

Teague walked to the window and looked out into the street. He stood silent, silhouetted in the sunlight coming through the window. When he spoke his voice was low, soft yet stern.

"I know you have had a helluva time, son. Nobody is doubting that. But there has to be more to your life than thinking about killin' people who wrong you. If that's it, you will never be able to kill enough to satisfy you."

Getting no response, Teague looked back toward the bed. Johnny was sound asleep. Teague quietly left the room not wanting to wake the boy.

17

A week later, although still sore and tender in some areas, Johnny was up and moving around. Miss Tucker kept wanting him to go back to school. Johnny had no intention of ever returning to school again. He didn't know what he would do, but he would think of something rather than going back to that school.

He was walking down the street thinking of his limited options. He knew Miss Tucker would keep pushing for him to go to school, he also knew that despite his young age, he would not give in.

He turned down the alley between two businesses. The alley was only a little cleaner than the muddy, urine filled street he had been walking down. Trash was strewn on the ground of the alley, and it smelled of rotting food and other things Johnny couldn't identify.

A noise in front of him caused him to stop. He could feel his heart racing in his chest. Since the beating he found himself scaring easily, a situation that he despised.

He saw someone rummaging through the trash just ahead of him, though he couldn't see who it was. Only a big guy, dark skinned.

The man must have heard or sensed he was not alone in the alley. He sprang up to his full height and looked toward Johnny.

Johnny saw it was his friend, Tom. Tom shook his head when he saw the boy.

"Yous scared me, boy. Thought yous the marshal," Tom said as he walked toward Johnny.

"What are you doin' back here?"

"Oh, I's just…" Tom looked at Johnny's bruised face, then made a sound in his throat. "Your face is healin' up, Johnny Cole?"

Johnny looked down at the ground, embarrassed to face Tom.

"They tricked me. I couldn't fight back."

"Fight back? You even know how to fight?"

Johnny shook his head.

"I stay outside of town, me and the wife do. Come with me and I show you some things. May he'p or may not."

Johnny was confused for a moment trying to sort things out on his mind. Finally, he looked at Tom.

"Mr. Tom? I figured you for a slave. Though I don't know much about what that is. But you are a nigger, and I thought all niggers were slaves."

Tom looked down at the young boy for a long moment, then said,

"Yeah. I was. For a bit. I gots my freedom when my master died a few years ago. Most white folk don't like it. They are several of us that live over out of town a bit. Got our own people to be around."

"I don't know much about slavery. I'm ignorant of the situation, though I think that's why my folks were killed."

"They was," Tom said walking toward the rear of the buildings.

Johnny ran to catch up to Tom, falling into step with the bigger man.

"How do you know that?" he asked, looking up at Tom.

BIRTH OF A GUNMAN

"Folk talk a lot. 'Specially in front of a darkie they think is too dumb to know any better."

Johnny was confused; he seemed to stay that way nowadays. He shrugged, looking up at Tom.

"Marshal Teague seems to want me to forget about my folks killin'. I can't though. I swear I'm gonna kill the men that caused it."

Tom looked down at the boy and smiled.

"That's a heap of killin', boy. It's more than just the men who did it, too. It's the men who support the men who did it."

Tom patted Johnny on the back with a big, calloused hand, smiling down at him.

He nodded toward the west as he spoke,

"You come out to my place; meet the wife and my kids. I'll teach you how to fight back against some of these boys."

Tom walked off leaving Johnny standing in the back of the alley alone. Johnny wondered what an old black man that once was a slave could teach a white kid. In the end, Johnny decided it didn't matter. Tom was his friend.

18

The next few weeks Johnny visited Tom and his family at their little shanty house just west of town. Tom had two kids, a girl around Johnny's age and a boy a few years older. Johnny never failed to visit where he wasn't made to feel welcome, despite him being nervous the first few times he was there. The several people Tom had mentioned that lived close by were his brother and his wife. Johnny didn't have much to do with him, he seemed to hate everyone.

Tom's son, Marcus, always had his chores to do and as Johnny helped him, they struck up a fast friendship. It was while helping with the chore of unloading a wagon that Marcus, sweat soaking his thin shirt, looked at Johnny. Johnny felt the eyes on him; eventually he looked a question at Marcus.

"You the only white kid we know. You know that?"

Johnny shrugged.

"You are the only blacks I know, so I guess we are even."

Marcus grinned,

"Yeah, even. We could both be hung up if others knowed."

From behind them they heard a soft giggle. Johnny turned to see Lula, Marcus's sister, watching them. Marcus groaned in his throat, pointing toward the house,

"Lu, get back to the house. Ma will skin you and me alive she finds you out here at the barn."

BIRTH OF A GUNMAN

"I didn't know Johnny was here," she said, staring at Johnny with her dark eyes and smiling.

Johnny ignored her, in part because he didn't like her. She always seemed to be underfoot when he and Marcus were doing chores or playing games.

Marcus shook his head.

"He's always here. Now git on back to the house."

Lula stood a moment staring at the two boys. She stuck her tongue out at Marcus, turned on her heel, and ran back toward the house.

Marcus watched her go, and then looked at Johnny.

"Sorry."

"It's okay. Girls are a nuisance."

"You are over here a lot. My uncle thinks it's a problem."

"Your pa is teaching me to fight," Johnny said looking at Marcus.

It was true. Tom had been teaching Marcus and him how to fight. Tom had said nobody should be afraid of trash like that Phillip boy again. Johnny was determined to learn how to protect himself from the Phillip's of the world, so he threw himself into the lessons the big black man taught him.

Marcus was older and knew more about fighting than anyone Johnny had ever met. It didn't take long for Johnny to realize if he went into a fight with more than one opponent, it would be Marcus that he wanted standing next to him.

Johnny looked at Marcus a moment, thinking of what to say next, then said,

"Your uncle doesn't like me much."

"Unc don't like nobody that ain't our kind. You too white for him to like you."

"I can't change that so I guess I will just stay away from him."

"Why you wantin' to fight so bad anyways?"

Marcus went back to unloading the wagon, Johnny was leaning against the side of the wagon watching him.

"Phillip. I don't know his last name, can't recall hearing it. He gave me a whippin' a while back. I will never have that happen again."

Marcus put down the sack he was holding and looked at Johnny.

"If'n it was me I'd not waste time learning hand fightin'. I'd get me a gun and settle it like that. No man would lay hands on me again 'fore I'd shoot him down."

Johnny said nothing. He considered what his friend said, knowing he still had his father's heavy pistol hidden away at Miss Tucker's place. He just hadn't had the money to buy the caps he needed to continue target practice with it, though he did practice aiming and holding it every night.

Soon though, soon he would be strong enough to hold the gun proper and shoot it.

He noticed Marcus looking at him strangely.

"What?" Johnny said.

"You smilin' like you know somethin' I don't."

Johnny said nothing.

Part II

1861

19

Johnny ran to get out of the winter rain. The wind caused the rain to hit with a force that felt as if his face were being stabbed by a dozen needles. He made it to the overhang of the general store.

He stopped to catch his breath for a moment, dreading going into the store and facing old man Kline. Since the summer he had been working in the store to help ease some of the debts Miss Tucker had piled up while keeping him and the other kids she took in.

Working in the general store allowed Johnny his own money to use and not have to rely on Miss Tucker for everything. It also allowed him to buy powder and balls for his gun which allowed him to practice shooting any chance he got.

Johnny pushed open the door to enter the store. Kline was sitting at the counter, one hand under his chin, reading a newspaper. He looked up as the door squeaked.

"Close the damn door, pup," he said, looking back down at the newspaper.

Johnny closed the door hard, causing the glass in it to rattle.

"I don't know of another way to get inside the store," he said.

Kline was pushing sixty and was always grumpy. Johnny at first had been intimidated by his gruffness, but as time went on had learned that if he responded with gruffness of his own then Kline was more than likely to leave it alone.

Kline stared at Johnny as he crossed the room.

BIRTH OF A GUNMAN

"You damn orphans are gonna be the death of me yet."

"Mr. Kline, I reckon there is a whole list of people who will raise a celebratory drink when you do kick the bucket. I will be the first, I can tell you that," Johnny said, putting an apron on and tying it behind him.

Kline grunted at Johnny as he glanced up at his young employee.

"You're a nuisance is all you are, boy. I could find better help than you any day."

"I can't wait for that day, Mr. Kline. I will gladly give them my apron."

"While you're waiting, go fill that order on the other cabinet for Goodson. He'll be here in a little bit. Don't keep him waiting," Kline said, not looking up at Johnny.

Johnny walked to the counter slowly. Goodson? It would be the first time Johnny had seen him since he had stolen the horse from him. Johnny was too embarrassed to go anywhere he thought Mr. Goodson would be. Now he was coming to the store and Johnny had to fill his order.

Pleading with Kline to fill it instead would do no good. Kline was not a very tolerable person and he seemed to have no tolerance for Johnny at all.

Shrugging it off, Johnny went about filling the order and placing items in a burlap sack for easy carrying. He was nervous about seeing Mr. Goodson again, the fear coming from the fact that the Goodson's had been good to him when his folks had been killed, and Johnny repaid that kindness by stealing their horse.

The bell above the door rang out, Johnny turned to see Mr. Goodson coming into the store. The wind was blowing hard and cold as he closed the door and looked around. He noticed Johnny behind the counter across the room from the door. Kline was still reading the paper.

"Johnny Cole, how are things with you, boy?" Goodson said, watching Johnny.

"Just fine Mr. Goodson. How is Mrs. Goodson?" He tried to keep the nervousness from his voice.

"She told me you was working here now. Old Kline couldn't find better help, I guess," Goodson said as he walked to the counter where Johnny was.

Kline raised his head and looked at Johnny for a moment.

"A better hand I could only hope to find, Goodson. He should have your order filled in a jif."

Goodson glanced back over his shoulder at the storekeeper. Johnny placed the sack in front of Goodson, shocked that Mr. Kline would say such a nice thing about him to the man.

"What's in your craw, Kline?" Goodson asked as he lifted the sack from the counter.

"War, by God. Don't you read the papers?"

"It's all old news by the time it gets here, I guess."

"This is this week." He slapped his hand on the paper he was reading. "Came in on the stage this morning."

Kline lifted the paper and shook it at Goodson.

"They done gone and called for a convention to vote on secession. The country is goin' to hell for sure now."

Kline threw the paper down on the counter. Goodson laughed a small laugh.

"They want slavery, Kline. Other than Johnny here I guess you never had no slaves."

BIRTH OF A GUNMAN

"Figures you'd be a secesh man. You always was, too. Was always a wonder to me why you took this boy in when his folks were kilt by the very people you agree with," Kline said, pointing a finger at Goodson.

Goodson glanced at Johnny, placed money on the counter in front of him, lifted his sack, and left. As Goodson left, Johnny was left with more questions than he had ever had.

20

"What did you mean by that, Mr. Kline?" Johnny asked, stepping out from behind the counter to stand in front of his boss.

Kline looked at Johnny a moment, he seemed to slump a little as he stood there. He took a deep breath then walked to the front window, staring out into the rain-soaked street.

"You like Miss Tucker, Johnny?" he asked, not looking at the boy.

"Sure. She takes good care of us boys. Some just pass through though."

"You stayed though, didn't you?"

"I did. I have nowhere to go. Some of the others had family or they just left. Like Phillip. He works on a spread now."

"He visit any over at Miss Tucker's?"

Johnny shook his head.

"I don't think he likes Miss Tucker very much. He was always mean to her."

"He was mean to you too as I recall."

Johnny didn't know how to respond to that statement, so he changed the subject. He wanted to know more about the war talk that the paper had been talking about.

"What does all this talk of war mean, Mr. Kline? And how long will it last?"

BIRTH OF A GUNMAN

"Who knows. All I know is that people like Bill Snyder and Mitch Goodson have been pushing for war for a while. They don't care who gets hurt in the process."

"Snyder killed my ma. I saw him do that."

Kline turned and looked at Johnny.

"You tell Teague?"

Johnny nodded. Kline waited for Johnny to continue.

"The Marshal said there was nothing to be done about it."

Kline made a noise in his throat but said nothing.

"When I grow a little, I aim on doing something about it, though."

"Grow? How old are you now?"

"Soon to be Fourteen."

"You are as tall as most men now. But you can't hang on to anger all your life Johnny. It's not normal."

Johnny shrugged a shoulder but remained quiet. Kline looked out the window again, lost in his own thoughts. He sighed.

"Better be thinking on something Johnny."

"Like what?" Johnny was in mid turn to go back to the counter. He stopped and looked at Kline.

"Whether you are fighting in this upcoming war or not."

"Maybe it won't last long. Maybe I won't have to decide."

"Goodson and others think that as well. Goodson is a damn fool, son." Kline turned from the window and walked back to his counter. "This war will cost us a lot. Money, lives. Damn shame, too."

"I got no reason to fight."

Kline looked over at Johnny and smiled. It was a tight smile, full of sadness.

"Reason will have little to do with this, Johnny. This will be friend against friend and neighbor against neighbor."

He straightened from where he leaned on the counter.

"Time to run on home. I'm closing early to see what is going on in town."

Johnny was confused. Kline never closed early. And he never let Johnny out of work early either. He took his apron off and set it on the counter.

He left the store not knowing where to go next. He decided at the last minute to visit Marshal Teague. The rain had let up though the wind was cold. He huddled in his jacket for warmth. As he was crossing the street, he could hear loud voices from the saloon. He stood in the street, watching the men crowd the boardwalk in front of the saloon. Each man trying to push his way closer to the door, yelling at the man behind him.

Johnny walked over slowly and stood in the dirt street just off the boardwalk. He looked at the man next to him.

"What's going on?"

The man looked over at Johnny, smiling.

"We are gonna burn out the darkies that live out on the edge of this town. That's what's going on. You gonna witness us take our town back from the them people."

Johnny didn't know what the man meant by take the town back. Tom and his family were the only black family in the area, he stared at the crowd a moment, then looked back at the man.

"Take it back from what?"

The man ignored Johnny. After a few minutes, Johnny turned and ran toward Miss Tucker's. He needed to get some things together and try to warn Tom and his family.

BIRTH OF A GUNMAN

21

Once in his room, Johnny could think of nothing he needed to gather, except for his gun. He went to the wall by the window, kneeled and moved the loose board.

The gun was there along with the powder and caps and balls that the big gun required to fire. Johnny put all the items in a leather pouch he had purchased from the general store months before.

He didn't know why he wanted the gun, but he knew the group of men at the saloon had guns. He tucked the gun behind his waist and covered it with his shirt.

As he came downstairs, Miss Tucker was waiting for him. Standing with her was Chad.

"Johnny, Chad told me what is happening in town. You can't go and warn them. It is too dangerous."

"It's dangerous for them too, ma'am. And they did nothing to deserve to be burned out."

"Those men will kill you," Chad said. "And if they don't, you won't be able to show your face around town if you help them people."

Johnny faced Chad, he was shocked to see he was taller than the other boy by a few inches, he never considered he wasn't the same boy they had beat up a couple of years before.

"At least you admit they are people. I could care less about the people in this town who would harm an innocent family."

BIRTH OF A GUNMAN

He stepped around the two toward the front door. He looked back at the two.

"Ma'am, you have been real good to me. I owe you a lot. I have to do this. They are my friends."

Miss Tucker nodded, then stepped forward to hug Johnny. She stepped back, tears in her eyes.

"You do what you need to. Be safe Johnny."

Chad laughed and shook his head causing Johnny to look at him. Without another word Johnny left the house unsure if he would ever be back.

Since he didn't have a horse, he took off walking and half running toward Tom's place. The whole time he was hoping he wasn't too late or that the men from town would not catch up to him.

He was happy to see the houses come into view. They looked peaceful sitting in the evening sunlight, wet from the winter rain, and warm as the chimney smoke rose in the sky. The shack houses looked like they were welcoming visitors. Johnny feared the kind of visitors that were coming.

As he made his way toward Tom's house, as he was approaching the uncle's house, he saw nobody outside. It was so quiet Johnny could hear his footfalls on the dirt.

"Stop right there, boy."

The voice came from behind him, scaring him a little. He turned slowly to see the big man. The uncle that didn't like Johnny at all. He was holding an old shotgun, pointing it right at Johnny.

"Where's Tom?" Johnny asked, determined not to let his fear show.

"Where he should be. Why you here?"

"To see Tom or Marcus."

"We ain't got time to play nice with the local white boy. I should kill ya now. That way the town folk know we serious too."

"I came to help you. To warn you."

Johnny felt panic for a moment. He didn't know the uncle's name, he thought it was Joe, but Marcus and Lula always referred to him as Unc, but he felt sure he was in danger. Despite the cold, sweat was rolling down his back and his face stinging his eyes, but he dared not move to wipe his eyes. He stood still.

From around the house came a voice that Johnny recognized and was happy to hear.

"Put that gun away. Johnny is a friend, and we need friends right now."

Tom came walking up to Johnny and stood in front of him, putting himself between the shotgun and Johnny. The uncle lowered the shotgun and walked up to Tom.

"He shouldn't be here, Tom."

Tom was looking at Johnny and grinning.

"Why are you here?" he said, still smiling.

"The men in town. I heard talk of them coming out here to burn you out or maybe worse. I didn't understand all of it, but I knew I needed to warn you. That's why I'm here."

"We already heard of that. We was in town earlier this morning."

Tom placed a big hand on Johnny's shoulder and squeezed lightly.

"See Joe, I told ya, Johnny Cole is a friend to the niggers. Let's get into the house 'for the real bad men show up."

BIRTH OF A GUNMAN

Johnny followed Tom and Joe into the house. He glanced toward town to see if he could see any sign of approaching horses.

22

Once inside the house, Johnny took a moment to let his eyes adjust to the gloom. He glanced around the small one room house that Joe and his wife lived in. Everyone was crowded around the lone table in the center of the floor.

Marcus, Lula, the wives, and now the three of them made the room seem even smaller.

Lula stared at Johnny with big brown eyes. Johnny knew Lula liked him, she had since their first meeting years ago. Lula was growing into a woman and did not resemble the little girl she had been back then.

Johnny caught himself glancing at her often. She was beautiful to Johnny's way of thinking. Each time he looked her way she was looking at him, a small grin on her face.

Tom's voice interrupted Johnny's thoughts.

"How many men in town were making trouble talk?"

"I don't know," Johnny shrugged. "Enough to wipe you out if they come here."

Tom nodded. Joe shook his head.

"What we gonna do, Tom?" Joe said.

"This is our home. We will fight for it."

"Can't we make a home somewhere else, Tom. This is crazy to die for a shack in a town that nobody wants us in," Tom's wife said.

"Ma'am, if I may," Johnny said. "I don't know much about this war talk that's been going on for as long as I remember. But my thinking is that nowhere is going to be safe for a long time."

"Nowhere for us niggers, right?" Joe said.

Johnny looked at him.

"Or the whites who help you. My folks were killed because they believed slavery was wrong. They were against secession. I don't know what I believe yet, but I know you are my friends and I'm standing with you."

Joe laughed, loud, then looked at Johnny.

"Well, hell. I guess we win then. We got us a white orphan on our side fightin' for us."

"Enough, Joe," Tom said. "We don't have anyone else, white, orphan or not, he came out here to warn us and help us. Johnny Cole will do just fine."

Lula grinned at Johnny, causing him to blush. He felt the fire on his face. He hoped no one else noticed it. Lula was growing into a woman and Johnny could feel things when he looked at her that he never felt before.

Johnny reached under his shirt, pulling the big gun from his waistband. Marcus stared at the gun as Tom looked at Johnny and whistled softly.

"That's a big gun. Is it loaded?" Tom said.

"Yes, sir. I'm going to load the sixth shot now," Johnny said as he pulled the pouch containing the powder and balls from his pocket.

Joe and the two wives continued watching out the window as Johnny went about loading the gun. Tom picked his shotgun up from the table where it sat, Joe still held his in one hand down by his side.

"You know the folk in town ain't gonna treat you the same they find out you was out here with us," Joe said, not looking away from the window.

"You..Well, at least Tom and Marcus are my friends. I feel this is what I should do."

Joe turned to look at Johnny a moment, then said,

"Either way, folk don't cotton to us much. That will leave a mark on ya."

Johnny finished loading and put the pouch back in his pocket. He went to stand by the window next to Joe. He nodded toward town.

"I know of at least two men in town that had a part in killing my folks. I know what secesh means now. I didn't then. Ma and Pa were killed because they disapproved of secession. I aim to set that right."

"How'd your folks feel about owning slaves?" Lula asked.

Johnny turned and looked at her for a moment. She was sitting in a chair at the table and if Johnny concentrated hard enough, he could see the woman she was to be. He was almost speechless when he thought of that.

"I don't know how they felt on that topic, Lula. But I know that I believe no one should own another human."

Tom laughed a short laugh,

"We is fixin' to fight a war to find out."

"The war isn't going to be just over slaves. At least that's what most people say," Johnny said.

Tom's wife spoke up and said to all the men,

BIRTH OF A GUNMAN

"That is what it will be about, no matter what anyone says. Or how they may think it starts. It's about slaves. We are nothin' but property."

23

The men were sitting on the porch while the women prepared supper. The cold wind continued to blow, and pools of water made the yard a muddy mess. The men, Johnny was shocked to think of himself as a man, gathered close to the house to try to get out of the wind. They all watched the trail toward town.

"Tom?" Johnny said. "Can I ask a hard question?"

Tom glanced at Johnny a moment, then nodded his head.

"Where was you a slave at?"

"We was back east. A town called Nacogdoches."

"What was it like? Being a slave?"

Tom was quiet for a long time. He stared out into the muddy yard as the wind blew hard around the cabin.

"It was no life at all. We was property, owned. Like a man would own a shovel or a mule and when you was not useful anymore you were traded, whether you was old or young. If you's lucky they made you a house nigger, but I never knew but one of them. The beatin's you get for not working fast enough or workin' too fast. Never knowin' if the white folk were gonna come get your women for they ownselves.

One thing for sure though, Johnny. I plan on doin' my part to help the Union and maybe one day my kids and grandkids won't be under threat of the white men."

Johnny sat silent, not looking at Tom. Joe stood from his chair and looked over at Johnny, then back at Tom.

BIRTH OF A GUNMAN

"Don't be trustin' this white kid, Tom. He could be bringing them out here hisself. This whole thing could be a trap."

Johnny looked at Joe, and from somewhere deep inside himself he found the courage to speak up.

"Joe, I ain't part of nothin' except not liking a whole lot of people. Tom and his family is the exception. I like them. You, I don't cotton to too much, but if needed I'll do what I can for you."

Tom laughed as Joe turned to stare at Johnny Cole. Before anyone could say anything else, Marcus pointed toward the trail to town.

"Look, riders are coming," he said.

All eyes were on the trail as a group of six riders came walking toward the cabin.

Lula came outside to stand on the porch. Tom made her go back in the house, which she reluctantly did. A few moments later Johnny caught sight of her staring out the window so she could see.

Johnny's heart was pounding so hard in his ears he could barely hear any of the men talking. For all his talk, he hoped he had what it took to stand up to trouble. He touched the pistol in front of his waistband, it gave little comfort.

Tom saw him touch the butt of the gun, he looked at Johnny.

"You keep that pistol quiet 'til we see what they are about."

Johnny nodded, then Tom said,

"If you shoot, shoot to kill and take out the one that's the leader."

Johnny just stared at Tom.

The riders rode into the yard of the cabin, sloshing through the mud. They sat their saddles staring at the people on the porch.

One of the men pointed toward Johnny,

"I know that one. He lives at Tucker's place. He's an orphan."

Johnny surprised himself when he spoke up in his own defense.

"I'm an orphan because men like you killed my folks. I won't be forgetting that."

The man and his companions all laughed except one man. He gave a look to the group, and they all fell silent.

Johnny heard Tom whisper beside him,

"You know who the leader is now."

Tom and Joe both moved to the front of the small, cramped porch forcing Marcus and Johnny to take a step back.

Johnny glanced back toward the window where he had seen Lula before. She was not there.

Tom's voice caused Johnny to look toward the danger again, he stepped up beside Tom.

"You ain't welcome on our place, so just get to ridin'."

"Your place?" the bearded leader said. "You got things backwards, nigger Tom. Let me see if I can help you get your bearings. This is Texas and Texas is goin' to split from the union, you know the union that says we shouldn't own a few of you niggers. So, what is gonna happen is you and your people are gonna pack up and be gone in say the next ten minutes or we are gonna kill you. And this white orphan too."

The man looked over at Johnny smiling, then said,

"How's that suit you, boy."

Nobody moved or spoke. Tom stood still; Johnny stared at the men; Joe moved toward the door of the cabin.

"Don't move," the leader said, reaching for his pistol.

Johnny saw the movement, his heart pounding in his ears.

24

He didn't remember reaching for his pistol that was tucked in his front waistband. He only remembered the recoil as it bucked in his hand, and the smoke that blocked a clear view of the targets. He had practiced for so long, dedicating weeks and months, maybe years, to handling the Navy Colt that it felt natural to pull it out and bring it to action.

Johnny's first shot hit the leader in the face as he went for his pistol. The back of the man's head exploded, blowing pieces of brain and blood on the two men on each side of him.

Horses started bucking from the loud gunshot, Johnny shifted the gun and aimed for another rider. The gun bucked and the man fell from the saddle holding his side.

From the porch, Joe moved to the door of the cabin. He stood next to Johnny and Tom with the double barrel shotgun, he fired into the group of riders.

Some yelled, some cursed. All of them still in the saddle, spurred their horses out of the yard riding back toward town. As the gunfire quieted and silence returned to the cabin yard, Johnny felt he could hardly breathe, his heart was pounding so hard he was sure the others could hear it.

Two men lay in the dirt, one dead, the other wounded. He was moaning, tears in his eyes from the pain.

Tom stepped off the porch followed by Joe. Johnny and Marcus looked at each other then followed the older men.

Tom looked down at the wounded man.

"Why'd you come here? We did nothin' to no one."

The man gritted his teeth through the pain, he jerked his head toward the dead man.

"Jim wanted to burn out the niggers in case trouble happened here."

Joe kicked the man in the wound on his side. The man howled in pain and rolled onto his back.

"Trouble is here now," Tom said.

"I need a doctor or somethin'," the man said.

"What's your name?" Tom said.

The man looked at Tom then the rest of the group. He lowered his head onto the ground.

"Pete. Pete Denman."

Tom nodded.

"I'm Tom Sherman. And you picked the wrong niggers to attack Pete."

Johnny looked at Tom and Joe. He realized it was the first time he had heard their last name after all these years of knowing them.

Tom turned toward Johnny and Marcus, looking at Johnny a second longer.

"Marcus, gather up the two horses. Johnny can take Pete back to town along with the dead man."

As Marcus left to gather the two horses that had wandered off, Tom looked over at Joe then back at Johnny.

"Johnny Cole. Son, you are in some trouble now. The town will be after your hide for helping us. You were quick to shoot that man. You better be quick to shoot from here on."

Johnny could only nod his head. He felt as if he could not catch his breath. The next time he was aware of anything, Lula was standing beside him with a cup of water. He looked at her, she smiled at him.

"That was brave, what you did," she said, handing him the cup.

He nodded at her as he accepted the drink. The water was cold and tasted good. Lula turned and went back inside, Johnny watched her.

"Johnny, you have to take these men back to town. We will tie the dead man across the saddle of one horse and make Pete here hold him in place as you ride the other horse."

"Why me?"

Joe looked at Johnny and took a step toward him, Johnny stood his ground as Joe said,

"You kilt him, you take him. We can't."

The next thirty minutes was spent putting the men on the horse. Pete was sitting in the saddle, the dead man, Jim, was placed in front of Pete, his hands tied to the stirrups, then Pete's hands were tied to the saddle horn over Jim's body.

Pete's wound was bleeding again from the exertion of moving. Johnny took the other horse, noticing the holstered pistol that was tied to the saddle horn.

Tom walked up to Johnny as he settled in the saddle, he patted Johnny's leg.

"You be careful goin' into town. They will be more that support this man than will understand what happened out here."

"I'll go to Marshal Teague first thing," Johnny said, taking hold of the reins.

Tom shook his head,

RONNIE ASHMORE

"That marshal is no friend of ours. You watch yourself."

25

Once on the trail toward town, Pete became talkative. Johnny was only half listening to what was said until his pa's name was mentioned.

Johnny reined up, both horses stopping in the middle of the trial. Johnny's horse blew as it stood there.

"What did you say about my pa?"

The man looked bad, he was pale, breathing hard, and barely sitting in the saddle. Johnny figured if he hadn't been tied on, he would have fallen off.

Pete looked at him, a smile played on his lips.

"Bill was his name, right? He was goin' around talkin' of how secession and splittin' from the union wasn't the answer. He also thought slavery was a bad thing."

"It is a bad thing."

"It's in the Bible boy. How can that be a bad thing?"

"I don't know much about the Bible, but I know a bad thing when I see it."

"Oh, you'll see it when we get to town then if that's how you feel. Ain't nowhere in town safe for a nigger lover like you. Teague won't help you, hell it was his idea to go burn them out. Jim was just the one who volunteered to do it. Along with the rest of us."

"What do you mean?"

Pete coughed up blood, and some fell onto his hands tied in front of the horn of the saddle. He looked at it for a long moment, then said,

"I guess I'm dead anyways, huh. Might as well tell ya."

Johnny was losing patience with the talkative prisoner.

"Tell me what?"

"The truth. Seems no one has done that to you yet. They's a whole passel of people in town that was behind the death of your folks. Not just Bill Snyder and Rick Palmer, but others who you would never consider. Secesh men all the way. Supporters of the war talk, unlike your pa."

"People can support what they want. I just want the ones who killed my folks."

Pete laughed, then winced from the pain, but continued laughing.

"Hell, boy, they been right in front of you this whole time."

"Who?"

Pete laughed again. Johnny dismounted, pulling his pistol from his waistband as he did so. He looked at Pete, who stopped laughing and was sitting in the saddle watching the young man.

"Tell me who they are, the ones who killed my folks and the ones who helped them."

"Why? What good will it do me?"

"I'll take you to town and get you a doctor."

Pete chuckled, moved his position in the saddle to ease his pain.

"I'm dead already son," he said, spitting blood on the ground.

"I need to know."

Pete looked around the area where they were, studying the trees as if seeing them for the first time. He shook his head and sighed.

BIRTH OF A GUNMAN

"Well, hell. You already know about Billy Snyder and Rick Palmer, but I bet you don't know that Mitch Goodson was one of them too. In fact, Goodson was one of the ones who made talk against your pa from the start. Then there's the marshal," Pete said, watching Johnny for a reaction.

Johnny stood still and tried to hide what he was feeling. Goodson and Teague were involved in his folk's death? Could that be right?

Johnny wanted to not believe the wounded man, but as he looked at Pete, he knew Pete was telling him the truth.

After a long silence, Johnny said,

"What about Kline? Or Miss Tucker?"

"Kline? No, he never cottoned to that bunch, but he didn't make it known either. That's why they...we left him alone. I don't know nothing about Miss Tucker except she's a pretty lady."

Johnny nodded his head, looking up at Pete,

"Was you part of the group that killed my ma or pa?"

Pete was silent for a moment, then shook his head.

"Not your ma, I wasn't there for that. That was Snyder and Palmer who led that group. The others are long gone from around here now. Only one I recall the name of is Ed. Newsome may be his last name. I don't know."

The man coughed again, longer and harder.

"But you hanged my pa?"

Pete nodded his head.

"Yeah. Me and Jim here," he nodded to the dead man tied to the saddle. "We did that along with Teague and Goodson."

"The Marshal? And Goodson, too?"

Johnny could feel tears welling in his eyes. He had been lied to for years, first by Goodson then the marshal. He fought the tears back. He could feel the weight of the gun in his hand. The click was loud as Johnny pulled the hammer back.

He looked at Pete, nodding, hoping his voice would sound strong as he spoke.

"I appreciate you telling me. Now I know."

Johnny lifted the pistol and shot Pete as he was starting to say something. The bullet hit Pete in the heart, he was dead before he slumped in the saddle.

26

Johnny rode into town just an hour before sunset. The horse with the two dead men tied to it followed his horse down the dirty street. Only a few people were out as he came riding down the main street. He watched for a reaction from anyone in the crowd.

After shooting Pete and on his way into town, Johnny decided what he needed to do. The anger and rage he was feeling grew stronger as he got closer to town. Now in the saddle and riding into town he had a plan.

He drew rein in front of the marshal's office. Teague came out and looked at him, then the two dead men tied to the horse he was leading.

"What's all this?" Teague said.

A small group of townsfolk gathered around the two horses. Johnny could hear whispers from some of the men.

"Your friends, Marshal," Johnny said so the onlookers could hear. "These two were part of a group of cowards that tried to burn out and attack the Sherman's."

Johnny dismounted slowly, keeping his horse between him and the lawman.

Teague was quiet as he looked at the two bodies. Johnny could see it on Teague's face, he knew. What Pete had said on the trail had been true. Johnny pulled his pistol as he stepped around the horse's head. He leveled it at the lawman's back.

Some of the crowd gasped causing Teague to turn around to face Johnny.

"What is this?" he said looking at the gun.

"This is for my folks who you helped murder. This is for the Sherman's who would have been murdered. Mostly, it's for the lies you told me all this time."

"You won't kill me, Johnny. If you do, there will be nowhere to hide, nowhere to run."

Johnny shot him. The bullet went high hitting the lawman in the throat. Blood spewed from the wound and Teague fell to the ground choking on his own blood, dying as he gasped for breath.

He died that way, clawing at the dirt as Johnny watched. Johnny stared into the crowd looking for any other dangers or people he recognized from the day his mother had been killed.

Shocked faces looked back at him. Johnny glanced at the three dead men. He had never fired a shot in anger until today and now three men were dead. Johnny felt no remorse about the men he had killed. Instead, he felt strangely alive.

Seeing no threat from anyone in the crowd, Johnny untied the lead rope from his saddle horn. He looked at some of the men in the crowd as he stepped into the saddle of his horse.

The men stared back empty eyed, some of the women were crying and hiding their eyes. Johnny reined around and headed toward Miss Tucker's to gather his few belongings.

Miss Tucker was waiting as he walked into the house. She looked at him, her eyes wet with tears. She came to him as he entered the main room.

"Tell me you didn't," she said, grabbing his arms.

He pulled away from her.

BIRTH OF A GUNMAN

"I did. And I liked it, they all deserved to die."

He pushed past her and went upstairs to his room. As he looked around, he realized he had nothing worth gathering up. He owned nothing, he cherished nothing in this world.

He heard a commotion downstairs. He listened to determine what it was. He heard voices. Someone was yelling at Miss Tucker.

Johnny came down the stairs slowly, listening to what was being said. He could hear a familiar voice telling Miss Tucker of how the marshal had been murdered on the street and someone should shoot Johnny down.

At the bottom of the stairs, Johnny could see Phillip, his old enemy, standing over a seated Miss Tucker. Phillip had not been around much lately as he had been doing ranch work for locals. He still came around now and then to mostly talk down to Miss Tucker or to try to bully some of the boys who lived with her.

Johnny stepped into the room, Miss Tucker gasped, and Phillip turned around to face Johnny.

"Why are you here Phillip?" Johnny said.

"Johnny, it's not what you think," Miss Tucker said as she stood up.

"You killed the marshal and two other men. What is wrong with you?"

Something cold turned over in Johnny as he looked at Phillip, remembering the beating he had taken from him when he first came to live with Miss Tucker.

"Those men were mean men. The marshal was a bad guy too. So are you, Phillip. You make Miss Tucker cry and treat her bad, treat the boys who live here bad. You're basically useless."

Phillip could see the look in Johnny's eyes.

"I'm unarmed."

Johnny shrugged.

"Not my problem, Phillip. I was unarmed that day behind the school, wasn't I?"

In a flash the pistol was out, and Johnny fired twice. The first bullet hit Phillip in the stomach, the second hit him in the chest.

As Phillip fell back and tumbled onto the floor, Miss Tucker screamed out.

"No…" tears filled her eyes as she looked at Johnny standing in the entranceway, the gun in his hand. "He was my son."

Johnny shrugged, turned, and walked away.

27

As the sun was setting Johnny took off out of town. He had no idea where he was going or even how to get there. He had never been more than ten miles from town in his life, now he was alone and probably would be a wanted man by daylight.

He headed east for no particular reason except that when the men left town they always headed east. He figured he would find a town somewhere up ahead.

As he rode along, he inventoried what items he had. The horse was technically stolen property, the saddle was in good shape. There was a long rifle in the scabbard, and the Walker Colt was in the holster still looped on the saddle horn.

He made a mental note to check the saddle bags for any useful items when he could.

Now, the only thing on his mind was finding a camp. Riding at night through unknown country did not sit well with Johnny. He needed to find a place to stop for the night.

It occurred to him he didn't know how to make a camp. He had lived in his parent's house, and then in town for most of his life except for the few days he had spent at his old house when he had left the Goodson's.

The Goodson's. How was he going to make Mitch Goodson pay for his involvement in the death of his parents? Johnny felt it needed to be set right, but he also knew he needed to get out of the area as fast as he could.

Once Goodson heard of what happened to his friends, and that Johnny had done it, there was a good chance he would look over his shoulder expecting trouble. That gave Goodson an advantage. Johnny decided to let it be for now. One day he would find him when he least expected it, then the advantage would be Johnny's.

Johnny came to a small creek that ran beside the trail he was following. He reined up and looked around. It would soon be dark, and Johnny wanted to be off the trail.

He followed the creek for a few yards, crossed over to the other side to find a spot to stay the night. He found a clearing among some pecan trees.

After the saddle was stripped and the horse tied to a tree for the night, Johnny realized he had no food, no water, and no way of starting a campfire.

This realization made him question what he was doing or was going to do for that matter. He couldn't read very well, couldn't write much more than his name, knew nothing of numbers, and had no skills that could earn him a living.

Other than some stolen guns, a horse, and three dead men he had nothing in the world to show.

Disgusted and feeling at odds with himself, he spread his saddle blanket and laid down for the night. It was cold but at least the rain had stopped. He was asleep before full dark.

The morning sun woke him from his sleep. It was a damp, soggy morning. Everything was wet. The pistol was wet as well as he picked it up and wiped it dry.

He was hungry but had no food. He rummaged in the saddlebags that laid beside him. There was nothing useful in them either.

BIRTH OF A GUNMAN

He slowly saddled the horse and rolled his blankets thinking of what he was going to do. He reloaded both pistols, the powder and the balls were in the saddlebag for the saddle gun. He stored both pistols in the saddlebags to keep them dry as the sky looked like rain.

He mounted and found the trail he had followed. He headed east again, not sure where he was going. One thing he knew, he could not spend another night like the last, cold, hungry, and wet. He needed to find a town and someone who would have mercy on a boy alone. Hopefully someone who had not heard that he had killed three men yesterday.

He had ridden for an hour waiting for the rain to start but it held off and the sun started to shine warming things up. Johnny was feeling good about his prospects of finding someone in town to help him then a thought struck him hard.

He would have to learn to survive without towns if he were to keep living. He had killed three men and would be wanted for that the rest of his life. He would need to stay in front of the hangman's noose if he wanted to grow older.

The thought seemed to knock some of the easy-going spirit from him. He turned and looked back the way he had come. He saw nothing, but he thought he could feel a posse closing in on him.

When he looked forward the way he was going, he reined up, staring at the man who stood in the middle of the trail pointing a rifle at him.

Johnny thought of the pistols in the saddlebags and wished he had them now. Another lesson learned the hard way.

The man was dressed in dirty clothes, threadbare and holes in the shirt, pants that looked greasy from being dirty. The man himself wasn't in any better condition. A long, stained beard that was starting to gray, hair in need of a cutting. The tall man was an imposing figure.

"Mornin', boy," the man said, cocking the hammer on the gun.

28

"Where ya headed?"

Johnny shrugged, "Don't know."

"Got any grub?"

"No."

The man still held the rifle toward Johnny, it was pointing toward the ground now.

"You're a kid. Why you out here alone?"

Johnny ignored the question, instead he asked one of his own.

"You gonna kill me or let me ride on?"

The man stared at Johnny a moment, then said,

"Ain't decided. Where you headed?"

"East."

The man lowered the rifle, smiling at Johnny.

"East covers a lot of ground, boy. Come on into my camp. I got coffee and a little grub," he said as he walked off into the wooded area off the trail.

Johnny dismounted and with reins in hand, followed the man into his makeshift camp. The cook fire was burning low, a coffee pot sat on a rock beside the fire. A pan was sitting just off the fire, the smell of cooked meat made Johnny's stomach grumble from the lack of food.

A piece of canvas was stretched between two tree branches creating a shelter for the man to sit under and keep dry.

Johnny took all this in as he tied his horse to a tree branch. He walked to the fire, kneeled, and began warming his hands.

"Johnny," he said, not looking at the man. "My name is Johnny."

"Okay," the man said. "You drink coffee? Here's a cup, pour you some."

Johnny took the cup from the man. He stared at it for a moment; it looked to have never been cleaned. Johnny poured himself a cup of coffee.

He had never had coffee before. Miss Tucker had never let him drink it. He took a sip of the hot liquid as his mind thought of Miss Tucker.

Phillip was her son? Was that why she put up with all his disrespect? It mattered little now. Phillip was dead and Miss Tucker was free of that burden.

The man's voice interrupted his thoughts.

"They call me Ned."

Johnny looked at the dirty man and nodded.

"What are you gonna do when you get east boy."

Johnny looked up at the man, then said,

"Name is Johnny. Not boy. I reckon I'm just driftin'. I got no place to go."

"You look like trouble to me. A young 'un out here on his own. No food, no water canteen. You're on the run from something or someone I figure."

Johnny sat silent. How did this man know that? Had word already spread of what happened back in town?

He shook his head slightly to clear his thoughts. No, that couldn't be the reason Ned said what he said. Johnny decided to probe a little more.

"Why say I look like trouble?"

Ned looked at him. His beard moving upward slightly, the only indication of a smile.

"I know things. I get notions occasionally. I got me a notion about you, Johnny," he said, handing Johnny a piece of the cooked meat.

Johnny accepted the meat quietly. It was the first food he'd had in a while, it tasted good to him. He ate it fast and washed it down with some coffee.

"You heading to a town, Ned?"

"Headin' to San Antonio to see if we are gonna fight or not."

"Are you wanting to fight?"

Ned was silent as he fiddled with the fire and the pan with the meat in it. Finally, he looked over at Johnny and shook his head,

"No. Reckon I'm not wanting to. Been fightin' Comanche for years, Mexicans too. I just want to know what is happening. They say slavery is wrong. I don't know about that, never owned any."

"Slavery is wrong, Ned. Nobody has a claim on another man."

"Maybe so. Most darkies I know ain't worth killin'. Damn sure ain't worth fighting a war over."

Johnny stared at Ned a moment thinking of the Sherman's. Tom, Marcus, and Lula. Lula, in Johnny's mind anyway, was damn sure worth fighting for. Johnny had killed for the Sherman's. He had no doubts he would kill again if needed.

"We disagree on that I guess," Johnny said, taking a bite of meat.

RONNIE ASHMORE

29

"How's that?" Ned said, looking around at Johnny.

Johnny sat on the ground chewing his food. He sipped his hot coffee to wash it down. He shrugged his shoulders and looked up at Ned.

"We disagree about the blacks. I think some of them are good people. They had a hard go of it so far."

Ned stepped closer to Johnny.

"A hard go you say. I should laugh or kick ya, boy, one or the other. The nigger has nothing going for him. If we win this war that they say is brewing they should be sent back to where they came from."

Johnny was unimpressed by the anger in Ned's voice. Instead, he smiled as he said,

"I know a black family and I don't think they'd want to go back to Nacogdoches."

"I ain't talking about no Nacogdoches. I'm talking about Africa."

Ned kicked dirt as he sat down. He looked over at Johnny as he pulled his hat off.

"Perhaps we shouldn't talk about this anymore. You're too young to have an opinion on this matter anyways."

Johnny smiled as he threw the dregs of his coffee into the fire. He looked over at the older man, deciding to change the subject.

"How far is San Antonio?"

"I'll be there by noon tomorrow, maybe a little past."

"Is it a big place?"

Ned looked at Johnny a long moment, then said,

"Fairly big. I have a notion about you. You're young but I believe you are on the run from someone."

Johnny didn't look at Ned, he got up and busied himself with unsaddling his horse. He laid his blanket out by the fire, sat down, and leaned against his saddle.

Ned watched Johnny work without a word. When the youngster was settled Ned scooted himself back under his lean-to shelter of canvass that was hung over some tree limbs.

"Gonna get cold tonight when that sun goes all the way down. May rain some too," he said, stretching out and laying down.

Johnny was quiet, knowing if the rain came, he would be soaked. He was hopeful the fire would at least keep him warm through the night.

"Might benefit you to get some supplies when we get to San Antonio otherwise you'll die out here before a month is up."

Johnny was alone in his thoughts for a long time, then he said,

"You ever hated someone before?"

Ned sat up on one elbow looking out at Johnny laying by the fire.

"You got you a hate goin' do you?"

"All my life."

"Well, that can't be all that long, judging by you."

Johnny raised up, turned to look at Ned.

"Have you?"

Ned cleared his throat, then said,

100

"Yeah. I've hated. When I was younger, now I live my life day to day and don't worry about people too much."

Johnny laid back down and was silent for a moment, then said, "I'm tired, scc you in the morning."

Ned laughed.

"In the morning everything will be a soggy mess, including you."

Ned's word was true to form. The next morning broke wet and muddy. The rain had started a couple of hours before daylight and fell hard and cold. The wind was blowing out of the north adding to the misery.

Ned was up making coffee, his makeshift shelter keeping him mostly dry, and the fire was built close to the opening keeping him warm.

Johnny was awake and miserable. He was cold, wet, and sleepy. He had no warm clothes, just the ones he was wearing which were threadbare and in need of replacing.

It was shaping up for a horrible day.

30

Johnny saddled his horse in silence while Ned gathered his things together. Johnny was perturbed; there was no offer of coffee, no offer of breakfast.

He could sense a change in Ned's attitude toward him, but he didn't know why. It was true the night was miserable and cold but Johnny had slept through it without complaint and had awakened to Ned being strange toward him. He'd had enough of it.

He reached into the saddlebags and felt the cold iron of the pistols stored within them. He looked over at Ned as he closed the saddlebag.

"Something wrong this morning?"

Ned looked over at him as he silently gathered his things together. Tying the canvass that served as his shelter to the back of his saddle, he spat on the ground then said,

"You. I thought on it last night. Whatever is doggin' you will most likely get me hanged. I ain't lookin' for a noose."

Johnny tightened the cinch on his saddle, he stepped into the leather.

"I'm not either."

Ned looked at Johnny but didn't say a word. Instead, he mounted his horse and led the way back to the trail, the horse's hooves slipping in the mud in places.

BIRTH OF A GUNMAN

Johnny followed behind, not liking the tone the morning had started on. When they reached the trail he moved his horse alongside Ned's, clearing his throat, he said,

"What do you do?"

"Little of everything. Though I'm getting too old to do much of that anymore."

Johnny didn't understand what that meant. He let it pass.

"I'm fourteen."

"Man enough I reckon to take on a man's work. I wasn't much older than you when I fought Mexicans at San Jacinto with ol' Sam."

Johnny stared at Ned a moment, then looked ahead. Ned had fought with Sam Houston, had been a part of Texas winning its freedom from the Mexican government.

"How does that feel? You fought for the freedom of Texas and now you're riding to show support for splitting from the union."

"We formed our own republic when we whooped the Mexicans. Now we are being dictated to from back east. I feel okay with it. Where do you stand?"

Where did he stand? Johnny had not thought much of the war talk except for the slave part. Was there more to it?

"I don't know. I ain't for slaves, I know that."

"You need to figure it out. You gonna have to decide sooner or later."

"They killed my folks about five years back, the secessionists did. My pa was not for splitting up. He said Sam Houston was right not to want that."

"Times change. It's gonna be hard to stay neutral in the coming years."

They rode in silence the rest of the morning. The morning started cold but warmed up as the day went on. Johnny was feeling the effects of the cold and could not wait to warm up by a fire and a nice meal.

The thought of food reminded him that he had no money. He thought hard on how to get some. He had nothing to sell except the extra pistol he had taken after killing those men. He wondered if he could sell it in town.

"You reckon I can sell a pistol when we get to town?"

Ned looked over at him.

"You got one to trade, do you?"

Johnny shrugged, not wanting to say too much.

They topped a rise and saw the town of San Antonio spread before them. It was the biggest place Johnny had ever seen in his life. As they rode down the hill toward town there were people everywhere. Wagons and horses scattered throughout the streets. The sounds of men yelling, women laughing, and people talking mixed with the noises from the stores and saloons created a mix of noise that overwhelmed Johnny.

They reined up in front of a hitch rail that stood in front of the general store. Johnny stepped from the saddle and stretched.

"Give me the gun you want to sell. I'll see you get top dollar and bring you the money."

Seeing the hesitation from Johnny, Ned said,

"It will be easier with me doin' it. Go on over to the restaurant over there," he nodded to a place across the street. "I'll bring you the money."

BIRTH OF A GUNMAN

Johnny reached into his saddlebag, retrieved the Dragoon pistol, and handed it to Ned. Johnny remounted and rode over to the restaurant.

31

After thirty minutes, Johnny was getting tired of waiting. How long did it take to sell a gun? Johnny didn't know since he had never sold one before.

Not for the first time the waitress looked over at where Johnny sat alone at the table. He had sat down anticipating a hot meal when Ned returned with his money. But all he had gotten was more hungry sitting at the table smelling the food odors and waiting.

Johnny stood and walked out of the restaurant, mounted up and went back over to the general store. Ned's horse was gone, not tied where they had parted company. He knew something was wrong.

He went into the general store only to find a lone old man sitting behind the counter. No one else was in the store. The clerk greeted Johnny as he walked in. Johnny stepped to the counter.

"A man been in to sell a gun in the last half hour?"

The clerk looked at Johnny a long time, then said,

"I mostly keep my business to myself. Why you asking?"

"It was my gun. A big, heavy colt."

"That fella said it was given to him. I traded for it. Gave him five dollars. You want it back I'll take eight for it," the clerk said, moving off toward a case behind the counter.

"Where did the man go?"

The clerk looked back at Johnny, snorted a laugh,

"I have no way of knowing. I assume with five dollars he went to find a card game at the saloon."

BIRTH OF A GUNMAN

Johnny turned and left the store. He took his pistol from the saddlebag, checked the loads, and put it behind his waistband. He mounted his horse and went in search of a saloon.

It was easy finding a saloon in the large town, they were practically lined up in a row down the main street. It proved harder finding the one that Ned might be in. An hour later, he found Ned in a saloon called the Alamo Saloon, not very original he thought as he read the sign.

Johnny walked into the bar and spotted Ned sitting at a table playing cards and drinking whiskey from a small glass on the table.

He walked up and waited for Ned to see him. Ned looked up for a moment. Johnny saw him pause just a moment then continue sipping his drink.

"You winning anything with my money?"

The men at the table with Ned stopped talking and began moving out of the way. One man laughed and said something about it being a kid. Johnny paid no attention to that. He was staring at Ned.

"Not your money, Johnny. I was unable to get a fair price for your gun," Ned said, not moving from his seat, just staring at Johnny.

"Clerk at the store said you sold it for five dollars. I'll take that and be on my way."

Johnny was scared. He could feel his blood rushing in his veins, and he had to force himself to talk slower to keep his words from coming out too fast.

"You calling me a liar, Johnny?" Ned said, an edge coming to his voice.

"I am."

"That's a harsh thing to call a man. If you were older, I'd kill you for that."

"I'm old enough, I guess."

Ned stared at Johnny for a long moment. Johnny could see him weighing his odds. He looked at the gun in Johnny's waistband, then to the onlookers staring at the two of them. Johnny knew enough about things to know there was no way Ned could back down from the trouble he found himself in. If he did, Ned would never live down the fact that he had been backed down by a young boy.

"Ned, I'm gonna ask one more time. Give me the money I'm owed, and I'll be on my way."

Ned stared at Johnny, then laughed a short laugh.

"Get on out of here, pup," he said, finishing his shot of whiskey.

"Johnny is my name. Johnny Cole."

"So? What does that matter?" Ned said, pouring another drink.

"I just want you to know who killed you."

Johnny pulled his gun and fired before Ned could react. The bullet struck Ned in the forehead knocking him back into his chair, where he slumped over. Dead.

The crowd was shocked at the sudden violence from the young shooter. Johnny looked at the men around the room. He went to the table, counted out five dollars from where Ned had his money laid out, then said,

"The man owed me money. Anyone have a problem with me taking what's owed?"

When no one said anything, he put the money in his pocket, the gun in his waistband, and left the saloon.

BIRTH OF A GUNMAN

32

Johnny was still hungry. He now had more money than he had ever had in his life. He felt rich. He rode over to the same restaurant, only this time he was confident he would eat well.

He walked in and sat down smiling at the waitress who had only stared at him earlier. She came over and he gave his order, including coffee, which he had developed a liking for since Ned had given him his first cup. Johnny smiled to himself as she walked away thinking it was the first decent thing Ned had done for him, and the last.

He paid his two bits for the meal, happy to have money left. He really had no idea what things would cost in San Antonio, but he needed some supplies if he were to be out on the trail in the cold.

That thought stopped him, the smile vanishing from his face. Where was he to go? He had no place to go to. He had no friends to speak of. He had killed five men now. The law would be looking for him.

There was a commotion on the street as men gathered around looking at the horse that was tied in front of the restaurant. His horse, Johnny realized.

Two men came into the restaurant, they stood in the entryway looking around the room. Spotting Johnny sitting at a table, they walked over to him and stood staring down at him while he ate.

BIRTH OF A GUNMAN

The two wore rough clothes that were no different than that of anyone else, but what caught Johnny's attention was the badges the two men were wearing.

Johnny looked up as he swallowed his food. The man on the right nodded toward the horse outside.

"Is that your horse outside?"

Johnny shook his head,

"No."

"Folks say they saw a young man riding it from the saloon."

Johnny said nothing, sipping his coffee.

"Man was killed over there at the saloon.

They tell of a young kid who did the deed."

Johnny could feel the heat start to rise in his face. He looked at the two lawmen, trying to find the words.

"He owed me money."

"Maybe you need to come with us. What's your name?"

Johnny stood, slowly so the lawmen would not get the wrong idea. The one who had not spoken reached over and took the gun from Johnny's waistband.

"Johnny Cole is my name."

The two lawmen looked at each other for a moment. Johnny thought he saw a flicker of recognition in the name. He was becoming more afraid as the seconds ticked by.

The two men were about the same height as Johnny, they stared at him a moment, then the quiet one said,

"Johnny Cole, huh? You wanted anywhere?"

Johnny shook his head,

"I'm wanted nowhere."

As the words left his mouth, Johnny knew a more truthful statement had never been spoken, at least by him.

The older lawman snorted a little laugh, then said,

"Act right and come with us. We will work out what happened at the saloon."

Johnny was feeling uncertain on what to do. He wanted to run but he was sure the two men would shoot him in the back if he tried. In the end he decided to go along quietly.

Once at the city marshal's office, which was housed in a building that sat in the middle of the block across from the restaurant, next to the general store, Johnny was led inside and seated in a chair in front of a battered desk.

The older lawman sat behind the desk while the younger one stood just behind Johnny, who fought the urge to look around at the man.

"My name is Lucas. I'm the marshal in town. What was the name of the man you shot?"

Johnny wasn't sure if Lucas was a first name or last. He decided to play it safe.

"Well, Marshal, his name was Ned. I don't know a last name for him. I met him on the trail into town."

"Trail from where?"

Johnny hesitated a moment, then said,

"I was riding in from Medina County way and met him last night."

Johnny briefly told the story of needing money and Ned's idea to sell the gun. After he finished the story telling how and why he killed Ned, he looked at the marshal.

"That's how it happened," he said.

BIRTH OF A GUNMAN

Lucas stood and walked behind Johnny to the other lawman, who handed Lucas the pistol they had taken from Johnny earlier.

Lucas handed the gun to Johnny.

"Can't fault a man, no matter how young, for defending his property and claiming what is his. You're free to go."

33

As Johnny left the marshal's office, he was counting his good luck. He had killed a man for five dollars and the law had said it was okay.

As he walked along the dirty streets, he thought how confusing the law was. Marshal Teague was a nice man who turned out to be a killer, while Lucas seemed like a tough man who had a soft side. It all was confusing to Johnny.

But not as confusing as hearing someone call out his name on the streets as he walked by. He looked for the source of the voice. People were everywhere, but he managed to catch a glimpse of the one yelling.

Johnny couldn't believe his eyes. Marcus Sherman was standing in the street near an old wagon, waving at him, trying to not be noticed by other white people on the street.

His black face broke into a wide grin when Johnny finally noticed him standing there. Johnny made his way across the dirty, muddy street to talk to his friend.

Lula was sitting in the seat of the wagon watching Johnny approach. When Johnny saw her he felt his heart beat faster. She was a pretty girl on the edge of womanhood.

He stopped in front of Marcus, tipped his hat to Lula, then said,

"What are you doing in San Antonio?"

"We came here so I could get in on fightin' the rebs, pa too, and Uncle Joe."

Johnny glanced up at Lula, then back to Marcus.

"What about Lula?"

Marcus laughed, shook his head.

"The women couldn't stay after what you did at our place. They would be in too much danger. So, they are all here too."

Johnny considered what Marcus had said, taking a glance around to make sure nobody was listening to them talk.

"What's the news from Medina?" Johnny said.

"The news is you are a crazy man who should be shot down on sight. The marshal and the two men you kilt ain't nothin' compared to you killin' that bully boy."

"Phillip," Lula said, looking down at Johnny.

Johnny glanced at her as Marcus continued,

"Yeah, Phillip. Folk mad about that as Miss Tucker is a well liked woman."

"They lookin' for me?"

"Don't you think they would be after what you did?"

Johnny was silent for a long moment, thinking about what had happened back in Medina. The killings of the men who came to the Sherman's house would be justified, but killing Teague and then Phillip would be looked on as murder. And they hang murderers.

Johnny shivered a little inside thinking of the hangman's noose. He decided to change subjects.

"Where are you staying?"

"By the river a ways," Marcus said, jerking his head toward the river.

Johnny nodded, then left his friends with a promise he'd come see them later. He took one last look at Lula before walking away.

She smiled at him, the smile seemed stiff and forced. It left Johnny confused.

He was walking down the street trying to avoid the mud and mire that the animals caused, when he rounded a corner and bumped into the marshal, Lucas.

For a brief moment Johnny was too surprised to speak, figuring the lawman was looking for him again.

"Johnny Cole," Lucas said, looking at the young man.

"Marshal Lucas."

Johnny tried hard to sound nonchalant. He hoped it worked.

"I've been looking for you. Let's go talk at my office."

Johnny definitely didn't want to talk to the lawman and especially at his office.

"Is there a problem, Marshal?"

Lucas smiled a thin smile, the mustaches rising on his face. It didn't seem genuine to Johnny but he really didn't know if it was or not.

"We can settle it in a few moments, I think."

Feeling trapped and with no other options, Johnny nodded and followed Marshal Lucas to his office. The whole way feeling like the ax of doom was about to befall him.

34

At the office, Lucas undid his gun belt and hung it on a peg by the door along with his hat. He sat behind his desk in the same chair he had occupied earlier. Johnny sat in the same chair he had earlier. They were the only two people in the small office.

"After you left, I heard a rumor," Lucas said.

Johnny didn't know if he should answer or not so he simply nodded.

"Medina? Tell me what happened there."

Panic hit Johnny fully then, he swallowed once and forced himself to calm down. He glanced at the door. Lucas leaned forward placing elbows on the desk.

"Tell me, Johnny. I can't do anything about it. Like I said, it was a rumor. And it is out of my jurisdiction. I have all I can do here in San Antonio."

"Sounds as if you know what happened."

Johnny hoped his voice sounded stronger to Lucas than it did to his own ears. He was scared but not wanting to show it.

Lucas must have sensed the young man's nervousness because he smiled at him, again his mustaches crawling like caterpillars on his lip.

"Relax, Johnny. I am not a Medina County lawman. Whatever happened there is of no concern of mine. My concern started and ended with the dead man at the saloon."

"Ned," Johnny said, though he didn't know why.

"If you say so. Tell me what happened in Medina."

Johnny tried to hold the lawman's stare but was unable to. Something about the way Lucas looked at him unnerved him to his core. As if he knew all the answers to the questions he was about to ask.

Johnny shrugged his shoulders, and looked down at the floor. He looked up and told Lucas everything. From the beginning.

Lucas listened without interruption or comment until Johnny had told his story, ending with meeting Ned on the trail to San Antonio.

When he had finished speaking, Johnny looked straight at Lucas, who only stared at the young man.

"That's a lot to handle at such an age, but others have had it worse. So in reality you have five dead men to your credit in just a few days span?"

The question rocked Johnny for a moment. He had never thought of the timeline of events like that before. Maybe because he was too busy being involved with living them.

"That's how it appears," Johnny said.

Lucas shook his head, leaned back in his chair, looked up at the ceiling for a moment. He then looked back at Johnny.

"You know war is coming to Texas right?"

"I know. It's about slavery and such."

Lucas leaned forward again.

"It's not slavery that we will be fighting for. It's the right to choose our own paths in deciding what our state should look like. Choice. Freedom to choose for ourselves."

Johnny remained silent. All he knew was that he was not supporting any war.

BIRTH OF A GUNMAN

"Anyway," Lucas continued. "The main thing I'm talking to you about is this. San Antonio as a town is split on the question of secession. The county is even more determined than the town to split. There will be a vote in a few days to determine what happens. I can tell you almost with certainty secession will pass."

"I could care less how anyone votes or feels. Secession men killed my folks. I will never be in that group for that and many other reasons."

"I'm not asking you to pick sides in the fight that's comin'."

"Then what?"

"I'm asking you to be my deputy."

Johnny sat there just as surprised as if he had been slapped. He could not have heard Lucas correctly. Deputy?

"A what?"

"When war comes it is going to take all the able bodied men with it. Including men that will be needed to fight Indians and outlaws and ne'er do wells. If you are my deputy then we can keep a lid on things here."

"Why me? I'm just fourteen."

"A fourteen year old who has killed more men in a week than I have in my life."

Lucas stood and came around the desk to stand in front of Johnny.

"What happened in Medina can either make you or break you. You kill easily, maybe too easily. But if you have the law on your side maybe you would be more cautious. I don't know. I do know I need people who can hold their own."

"I'll think about it and let you know."

Johnny got up and left the office dumbfounded that he had just been offered a job as a lawman. He stepped out on the street, collected his thoughts, then headed toward the river to see his friends.

35

"That's crazy. And unbelievable. He offered you a job?"

Johnny nodded at Lula and smiled.

"Are you gonna take it?"

They sat on the riverbank watching the water flow. The men were still in town tending to business, the women were in camp getting supper ready for their return. Johnny had been hoping to talk to Tom, but he had to admit sitting beside the river with Lula wasn't too bad either.

She was growing into a striking woman. It was hard for Johnny to remember they were the same age. She seemed more mature than he did, more sure of herself and of her place than he was.

Johnny looked at her sitting beside him, her gingham dress faded and threadbare, her brown shoes with homemade patches covering the holes in them, her dark hair pulled back in a horsetail. She had never looked so beautiful to Johnny.

She caught him looking at her and smiled.

"What are you looking at?"

"Nothing. Just thinking," he said, feeling embarrassed to have been caught staring at her.

"You gonna take that lawman up on his offer?"

Johnny shrugged his shoulders.

"What he said makes sense, with the war a coming and the menfolk leaving. But I'm young for lawin' don't you think?"

"You stood up for what was right at our place. No hesitation, no fear, least what I saw. You killed the marshal and that white kid for reasons of you own. And your friend on the trail that tried to steal from you. You seem to know right from wrong."

Johnny chuckled softly.

"I'm only fourteen. Who will take me serious as a lawman?"

Lula sighed, then adjusted her seat on the ground and started drawing in the dirt. Johnny watched her tiny fingers move back and forth.

"Is your pa gonna go fight too?"

Lula looked up at Johnny, tears filling her eyes, and nodded.

"Marcus and Joe too. They say it won't take long to whip 'em but I don't know."

"Nobody thinks it's gonna be easy, what I hear."

"Lula."

The voice startled them both. It came from behind where they sat. Johnny turned toward the voice and saw Tom standing there looking at them.

"Your ma needs you," Tom said, walking toward them.

Lula got to her feet, looked once at Johnny, then hustled off to her ma. Tom waited for Johnny to get to his feet before saying anything.

"You like my daughter?"

"Of course."

"More than a friend I mean."

Johnny was silent, looking at the big black man.

"This war that's comin' gonna be hell on the womenfolk," Tom said.

"You goin' to fight?"

"Yes sir. Joe is gonna go side with the Yankees. I can't abide that."

Johnny looked at Tom straight on.

"What?" he said.

"Yankees, fightin' with the yanks."

"You wouldn't join the Union?"

Tom looked at Johnny a moment, and then smiled, shaking his head.

"No. Only reason we is free is because my master got sick and freed us before he died. He was a mean ol' white bastard, but he freed me and the rest of us."

"I don't understand then."

"Johnny, It's a simple thing. Texas is my home. The only home I ever knowed. I never did go nowhere else. I aim to fight if'n war is comin' but it will be for Texas."

"But Texas allows slaves. How could you fight for something like that?"

"Ain't about slaves, son. It's about freedom to choose. A man should not tell another man what he can or can't do. Neither should a government tell another government what they should or shouldn't do."

Johnny was silent for a long moment; he looked up at the taller man.

"That puts you and your brother against each other."

Tom nodded, saying nothing in return. Instead, he gently touched Johnny's shoulder leading him back toward the campsite.

Johnny was silent the whole time, thinking about what Tom had said to him, trying to reconcile Tom's words with his parent's actions that had led to their death.

RONNIE ASHMORE

36

Johnny was still thinking about these things when he laid his bedding out by the fire. He had money for a hotel but he knew money would be scarce if he spent it on frills he didn't need. So he would stay the night in the Sherman camp.

The thought of money brought to mind the job offer from Marshal Lucas. Johnny wondered briefly if he had what it took to be a lawman, especially considering his youth. He could barely read, couldn't write very legibly, and never considered whether either of those things were of importance.

The idea of him being a lawman made Johnny shake his head in wonder. He had killed men recently. And he was only fourteen.

As he stretched out on the blanket he had borrowed from Tom he knew without a doubt what he would do. He wanted to get away from San Antonio as fast as he could.

He awoke before dawn, sat up in his blankets, and looked at the fire. It was cold. The north wind was blowing harder than normal bringing with it a coldness that seeped into a person's bones.

He managed to bring the fire to life as the womenfolk got up and moved around the camp to prepare breakfast. He watched Lula from the corner of his eye, noticing her looking at him as well.

She was a pretty girl growing into a beautiful woman. Her skin was dark and smooth; her lips were always smiling or grinning. Johnny had to look away and focus on something else.

That something else was getting his bed made as Marcus came walking over to him. Marcus stopped in front of a kneeling Johnny.

"You decided what you're gonna do?"

Johnny looked up at him.

"Lula told me of the offer to be a marshal. You taking it?"

Johnny stood and dusted his pants off with his hands.

"No. I can't say that it makes a lot of sense for me to take it. What about you? You still signing up to fight?"

"If they let me. I'll go."

"With Tom or Joe?"

Marcus was silent a moment, staring out in the distance of the fresh morning.

"I guess I can't fight for any place that allows slaves."

"This war seems a strange thing to me. Brother will fight brother, father against son, and for what?"

Marcus shrugged a shoulder then changed the subject.

"Where are you headin'?"

"I don't know. Medina maybe."

"Medina? Are you crazy? Why would you go back to Medina?"

"I dont know. I have no other place to go."

"No place is better than Medina, I can tell you that."

"I don't know. Like I said, I have no place else to go."

Johnny walked over to store his blanket in the bed of the wagon. Lula walked over to hand him a cup of coffee. Johnny took it and smiled at her, realizing for the first time he was not her height anymore, but rather taller than she was.

"Lula, what are you and your ma and aunt gonna do while the men are fighting?"

BIRTH OF A GUNMAN

"Pa says right here in San Antonio is safe enough for people like us. So, we are gonna stay here."

"By the river?"

"No, not by the river," she said, laughing. "Pa will find us a spot before he goes and fights the yanks."

"Marcus told me that him and Joe are gonna be joining those yanks. Aren't you worried?"

"Very much. I am worried very much."

Johnny said nothing else, instead choosing to just look at Lula and take in her features. She caught him looking at her.

"What is wrong?"

"Nothing. Nothing at all," Johnny said, smiling at her.

37

After breakfast Johnny walked back into town to the livery stable. He gathered his things and saddled up, the livery man watching him the entire time. Johnny could feel the old man's eyes on him while he worked. Finally, Johnny turned from his task of tightening the cinch and looked over in the corner where the older man stood.

"Is there a reason you keep looking at me mister?"

The old man stepped from the shadows, he spit tobacco juice into the dirt, then smiled at Johnny.

"I never seen no desperate killer 'fore," he said.

"How's that?"

Johnny turned to face the man full on. He felt the weight of the gun in his waistband.

"That's what the men who rode in this mornin' say about ya."

Johnny looked out the barn toward town, then back at the old man.

"What men? When?"

"They rode in 'bout daylight. Say they was lookin' for the boy killer who shot up their town then left headin' this a way."

"I guess you told them about the saloon shooting?"

"They's gonna find out sometime. They say you are a killin' sonofabitch. Four men in Medina, including the town marshal. That's some trail you left."

BIRTH OF A GUNMAN

Johnny led his horse outside the barn, looking the area over as he did so.

"Who were these men?"

"I don't know," the man shrugged. "One was dressed like townsfolk. He seemed to let the other one do the talking."

Johnny stepped into the saddle and adjusted his seat. He looked down at the livery man standing just inside the doorway.

"The talking one? He didn't look like a townsman?" Johnny said.

"No, son he didn't," the old man walked out into the sun. "He looked like a ranger to me. A killer hisself, I reckon."

Johnny said nothing. Partly because the words wouldn't come and partly because he didn't trust himself to talk. A ranger? On his trail. That could be bad.

Johnny spurred his horse heading out of town. He thought of the Sherman's for a moment. He wanted to see Lula again but he dismissed the notion from his mind. He had no right to bring his trouble to their lives.

Then a thought hit him causing him to rein his horse in hard. The Sherman's were in just as much trouble as he was. True it was him who had killed the four men in Medina. But it was the Sherman's who were the target of the attack that caused the killings.

Johnny knew enough about the rangers to know they would harass the Sherman's to get information on his whereabouts.

Johnny swore, loudly and with conviction.

If he went back to the Sherman's camp and shooting started, and if he wasn't killed in the process and if he killed a ranger, then the law would never stop looking for him.

His decision was simple, but tough to make. Maybe the two-man hunting party wouldn't find the Sherman's in town. Ride on and let the Sherman's handle what came. Or turn around and try to warn them of what he had learned.

He turned his horse around. He couldn't let the Sherman's carry his burden. And he didn't want Lula to be in danger at all. He would just ride by their camp, give a warning to them, and ride on north and disappear for a while.

He rode toward their camp with a wary eye open for any danger that may be around. San Antonio was a big town and there was always a mass of people on the dirty, muddy streets.

He rode fast but cautiously. In the trees along the river, he sat his horse and looked over the Sherman camp about twenty five yards away. Two men stood with rifles and the Sherman's lined up facing them.

One of the men had the women clustered together and was covering them with his rifle, the other had the men gathered and was covering them with his.

Johnny knew by the way they were dressed that the man covering the men would be the ranger. He listened hard hoping to hear what was said. The wind was blowing too hard for him to hear much except the general tone of the conversation.

It was decision time Johnny thought. Run and leave his friends or try to help where he could.

38

The decision was easy for Johnny to make. He eased back to his horse and took his rifle from the scabbard. He then returned to where he had been standing. Two against one sure didn't seem like good odds. Who to shoot first if he had to? Johnny wasn't sure how to decide that.

He watched from his covered position among the trees. The one man doing the talking was the one believed to be the ranger. He was yelling at the men and although the words couldn't be heard the voice could, and the tone along with his pointing indicated he was angry.

Johnny walked as quietly as he could out of the tree line to get closer to the men. He held his rifle ready to fire toward the camp, though he knew he wouldn't unless he had to. Too much risk of hitting one of the Sherman's. Still it made him feel better just holding it.

When he was twenty yards behind the two men he stopped. One of the Sherman's had to have seen him sneaking up but, if so, they gave no indication. Johnny brought the rifle to his shoulder, sighted in on the shoulders of the talking man.

"You move your dead," Johnny said.

The two men stood still for a long moment, finally, the quiet man said to the other one,

"That's him. That's the kid who killed the marshal and the other men."

There was a touch of fear in the man's voice. Johnny kept his focus on the ranger. If trouble was to happen it would come from him.

"So, you're Johnny Cole?" the ranger said, not moving.

"I am. And you're harassing the wrong people."

"Maybe not. Us being here brought your yellow hide out of the woods, didn't it?"

"Yellow? How you figure that?"

"You're a cold-blooded killer."

"I am just trying to survive," Johnny said, not liking the ranger's tone of voice.

The man had a rifle pointed at his back but was talking like he was in charge of the situation. Johnny glanced over at the other man, then back at the ranger.

"What's your name Ranger?"

"So you know who I am?"

"I know what you are. You're a man that can't find his target without harassing innocent people."

"I doubt you'd be so sure of yourself if you were facing me, young man. In fact, you are a coward in my opinion. Hiding among the trash that is this black family."

Johnny felt his anger rising toward the lawman. He wanted to tell him to stop talking but was afraid that would just encourage him to talk more.

The ranger laughed a little,

"You probably have a thing for the nigger girl, I would imagine…"

BIRTH OF A GUNMAN

Johnny shot him. In the back, the rifle report echoed along the riverbank. The ranger gave a short grunt; he fell to the ground dead. The bullet tore out the front of his chest.

The women screamed a short scream, and Johnny heard the other man gasp in terror. Not wasting any time, Johnny worked the lever of his rifle and pointed it at the other man.

"Look at me, mister."

The man turned slowly, his rifle held up in the air with one hand, he looked at Johnny. There was fright in his eyes, as if he were living his final moments. Johnny saw the look and somehow felt empowered by it.

"You got two choices. Ride on and forget you ever heard of Johnny Cole. Or die here, today."

The man nodded his head hard enough to knock his hat from his head. He made no effort to grab it as it fell to the ground.

"I'm just a storekeeper. The Mayor. The town wanted me to ride with him," he nodded toward the dead man. "I just want to go home to my wife and family."

Johnny lowered the rifle.

"Get goin'."

39

Tom Sherman stared at the dead ranger as Johnny searched the man's pockets for valuables. Tom took a couple of tentative steps toward Johnny, then went to his wife and daughter.

Johnny could hear them talking, asking about each other's well-being. He ignored the talk the best he could, he was focused on his task at hand.

"That gunshot gonna bring the law out soon or late," Joe said as he went to stand by his wife.

Johnny looked back toward town a moment, then looked at Joe.

"I got more bullets if he comes too soon."

"That's the man offered you a job lawin'," Tom said, stepping toward Johnny a step or so.

"Well, I guess I have to decline that offer now, don't I?"

"You ruinin' ever'thing you trying to do, boy," Joe said.

"It was ruined before I ever got here Joe."

"So, you just gonna go around killing people?" Joe said.

"They were threatening you. All of you," Johnny said.

Standing up, he pocketed the little money he had found in the ranger's pockets. Marcus and Tom were looking at him as if he were crazy. But Lula, she was looking at him as if he repulsed her. That look shook Johnny a little.

"That was just hot air. No harm could have come to us," Tom said.

BIRTH OF A GUNMAN

Johnny said nothing. He gathered the dead man's rifle and pistol. He wanted to try to explain himself to Tom and especially to Lula. But he had no time.

Joe was right. The gunshot would bring the law before too long, even though Lucas was town marshal. Johnny imagined he could hear the horse's hooves now as the lawman rode up the riverbank.

Whatever Johnny was at this, he knew he was no match for a man like Marshal Lucas. Not yet, Johnny thought. Someday.

He shook those thoughts from his mind as he stood and looked around. He looked at Lula for a moment and tried to smile at her. She turned and walked away from the group without a word or a look back.

He turned his attention to Tom.

"Nothing I can do about the body. When anyone shows up just tell 'em I was the one. It don't matter anymore now. Whether it's one dead man or six, it's all the same."

Johnny gathered his newfound items and turned to walk toward the tree line for his horse. Tom stepped toward him before he could walk away.

"Boy, you need to stay clear of towns and people for a long time. You kill some sorry town law, nobody gonna care much. You kill a Texas Ranger, they gonna hound you to Hell's gates."

Johnny looked at Tom for a moment, then said,

"Thanks for being my friend Tom."

"You welcome Johnny Cole. But stay away from my family from here on. You will bring nothing but trouble."

Johnny walked away feeling as if he had lost the only friends he had ever had or could ever count on. Tom was right though. It would be nothing but trouble for him for a long time.

Johnny walked to his horse, stepped into the saddle, and rode toward town, his rifle resting across his lap in his right hand, ready. If there were to be trouble from Lucas, it best be now instead of later.

As Johnny approached the main part of town, he could see men in the streets yelling at each other. Some appeared to be celebrating while others appeared to be at odds with the man next to him.

Suddenly gunshots rang out and men were yelling at top voice. Johnny took a firmer grip on his rifle and moved his horse forward along the already packed street.

Reining his horse in front of a small group of men who looked to be store owners, Johnny looked the street over, then asked,

"What's happened?"

One of the men looked up at him and said,

"Damn fools voted this morning in Austin."

They moved away as Johnny kneed his horse onward. So, it was happening just as old man Kline had said back in Medina.

Secession had come to Texas. War couldn't be far behind.

40

Johnny rode from town without looking back. He had no destination in mind, nowhere he wanted to go. He knew a lot of places he couldn't go, not anymore.

That thought brought up memories of Medina and his old home. He wondered if it was still standing or if the people who had hated his father had burned it down.

He shook his head to clear his thoughts. It didn't matter now. All of that was a long time ago.

He found himself heading north and he realized he had no idea what was ahead of him. He had no knowledge of towns or places that lay in this direction.

He chuckled to himself lightly. He would find out what all was out there in this world thanks to the owl hoot trail.

That made him consider a moment. He was near fifteen years old now and had a considerable number of dead men on his back trail.

Was that all his future held? He hoped not. He would like to settle down and try to have a family. Maybe with Lula.

Probably not. The way she looked at him after the killing on the riverbank let him know how disgusted she was with him. She had seen him kill before and while the first time she had said it was brave, this time her look said she was afraid of him.

His horse snorted and Johnny came back to his senses as the horse stopped in the middle of the trial. He looked up to see a wagon about fifty yards ahead.

The wagon was facing the same way Johnny was heading, he couldn't see who was in the wagon.

A head popped out of the covered rear of the wagon, a girl with her blond hair in horsetails. She stared at Johnny, then he heard her voice clearly,

"Pa, look there is a man behind us."

The man jumped from the wagon seat a rifle in his left hand, he motioned for the girl to get back inside. He stared out toward Johnny.

He was dressed in rough clothes, his dark hair was long, and his hat was pushed back on his head. He was tall, about six feet. Johnny could tell he was not an old man but rather young and big.

Johnny eased his horse forward walking it slowly to close the distance. He was trying to determine if the stranger was a threat or not. In this day and time, it was hard to tell.

He reined his horse in about ten feet from the rear of the wagon. The girl poked her head out of the canvass covering again. Johnny guessed her age was probably ten.

The man nodded a hello, then said,

"We can give you room to get by if needed."

"I'm in no hurry. Do you folks need help?"

The wagon rocked a little, and then a woman appeared from around the right side of the wagon. Her look, with her hair up in a bonnet and her dress made from homespun, instantly reminded Johnny of his own mother. She looked at Johnny a long moment.

BIRTH OF A GUNMAN

"We are heading north to some other place where we can get away from this war nonsense," she said.

"Mary hush, now," the man said, not looking at his wife.

"I guess I am doing the same thing," Johnny said.

"Forgive me, but you look so young. Why are you out here alone?"

Johnny smiled, shrugged his shoulders, and said nothing.

"Well, do you wish to accompany us for a while…What is it that I call you?" she said.

"Johnny, ma'am. My name is Johnny."

The girl giggled. The man looked over at her and she instantly disappeared into the wagon again.

"Don't mind her, she ain't seen anyone near her age in a while."

"How do you know how old I am?" Johnny said.

"Just a guess," she turned back to her husband, "We best be getting along, Walter."

The man stared at Johnny a moment longer, then turned and remounted the wagon. The wagon lurched then started moving slowly northward. Johnny followed behind wondering if the man knew where he was going.

41

As the miles past by, Johnny let his horse lag farther and farther behind from the wagon. Every so often the girl would stick her head out as if to make sure he was still following.

A few hours later, as the miles fell away, the man pulled the wagon off the trail into a clearing near a creek.

The woman got down off the seat and the girl jumped from the rear of the wagon. They both instantly started gathering wood for a fire.

The man loosened the harness from the horses, got a coffee pot, filled it from the stream and carried it back to where the women laying out the wood for the fire.

All of this happened before Johnny loosened his cinch. The man then led the horses to the stream to drink their fill. Johnny led his horse down to the water as well.

The two stood in silence for a moment watching the horses drink. The man looked over at Johnny and said,

"How old are you, boy?"

"Johnny. My name is Johnny."

"OK. How old are you, Johnny?"

"Almost fifteen."

The man grunted a little.

"So, you are fourteen."

Johnny said nothing as he watched his horse drink.

BIRTH OF A GUNMAN

The man turned and led his two horses back to the camp. Johnny watched as he walked off, he was uncertain how he felt about the man. Time would tell.

Johnny led his horse from the creek to a spot close to camp where he could stake the horse out. He finished stripping the saddle from the mount then walked to the fire as he caught the smell of the coffee making. The woman was already preparing a meal. Johnny felt a pang of guilt that he had nothing to contribute.

The girl was taking turns helping her mother and staring at Johnny. It made him a little uneasy the girl always looking at him like that.

The woman noticed her daughter's actions and looked at Johnny.

"Forgive her, she hasn't seen anyone her age or thereabouts in a long time."

Johnny tried to smile a non committed smile. He hoped it worked.

"The boy says his name is Johnny. Just so you wanted to know," the man said as he walked up to the fire and stood warming his hands, though it wasn't that cold.

The woman looked at Johnny and smiled.

"Johnny? That is a wonderful name. I'm Martha, the rough ol' bear of a man here is Jack, and this is our daughter Mary."

Johnny looked at each in turn as Martha announced the names. Jack never looked away from the fire as he said,

"Where you comin' from and where you headin'?"

Johnny knew inside he had a choice to make. Act like a fourteen-year-old kid and be intimidated by Jack. Or act like the killer he knew he was becoming and be tough. He decided to try a little of both.

"Where I have been is God's business. Where I'm goin' is the devil's," he said looking straight at Jack.

Jack met his stare, a smile played on the edge of his whiskered face.

"The devil will be here all right. I reckon this damn war that is comin' will se to that. You goin' to join up, Johnny?"

"This fight is no concern of mine. I don't even know what the fight is over. Some say freedom of states, others say slaves."

"Them fools voted for secession. They don't know what they are doing to this great state. It will hurt us all."

Martha interrupted her husband's talking,

"Let's not dwell on the bad, Jack. We are on our way to a better way. Far from San Antonio and the noise of war talk."

Johnny looked at Martha a moment. He was surprised they were coming from San Antonio as well. He decided not to mention anything about the town. Instead, he looked at Mary then back to Martha, and said,

"Ma'am, I been hearing war talk since I was younger than Mary there. I reckon the talk is over now."

42

The next morning was cold as the sun struggled to make an appearance through the clouds and drizzle. As the light rain had began falling during the night, Johnny only had his saddle blanket to cover with. The three others were tucked away in the wagon, warm and dry.

Johnny made a mental note to get some gear for the outdoors. He would most likely be spending a lot of time outside.

Martha was busy at the cookfire making breakfast. It was the smell of coffee that had awakened him.

As Johnny was pulling his boots on, Jack came out of the wagon and looked over at Johnny.

"Follow me to the water when you get your boots on," Jack said, walking off toward the creek.

Johnny took a little longer than needed in getting his boots on before going down to the creek where Jack waited.

Jack looked at him as he walked up.

"Which way are you headed?"

Johnny shrugged.

"I don't know. North is all I know."

"You heard Martha say we was comin' from San Antonio last night, right? I figure that's where you are coming from. I heard a story while I was there. About a boy killing a man in a saloon for five dollars. You hear that while you were there?"

"I heard it. The way I heard it told was the man tried to rob the boy of that five dollars. The boy was having none of it."

"They say he was calm and cool when he shot the man. I can see why since the man was unarmed."

"I believe he was armed. That is my recollection," Johnny said.

Jack was quiet for a moment, then said,

"Heard tell around the boy called himself Johnny."

"He called himself that because that's his name. My name. Johnny Cole."

Jack stared at Johnny. Johnny was surprised to see he could almost look the man in the eyes straight on. He had not realized how tall he had become.

"We are going to head toward Lampasas. Martha has kin there we are gonna stay with. Help out on their place and forget the war talk. You're welcome to ride along with us if you want."

"I may ride a little ways. The next town we come to I'll add to your grub."

"We got enough to get to Lampasas, so you don't have to if it puts you in a bind."

"No worries. I have a little under five dollars," Johnny said then turned and walked away from Jack.

At the fire, Johnny poured himself a cup of coffee and knelt next to the fire. The rain was falling harder, and it promised to be a miserable day.

After a quick breakfast, Martha and Mary cleared camp making sure everything was packed up. Jack hitched their horses to the wagon as Johnny banked the fire, he figured the rain would extinguish it fully.

BIRTH OF A GUNMAN

He saddled his horse and mounted as Jack snapped reins and started the wagon moving. They headed north in silence.

The day grew colder, and the wind brought an icy chill to the air. Johnny slouched in the saddle trying to avoid the wind. By the time Jack stopped for the noon meal Johnny figured he was near frozen.

Martha and Mary worked to get a fire going and the coffee making, the beans starting to roast in the pan.

She cast a glance at Johnny who was standing next to the fire trying to warm himself.

"You have any warm clothes?"

"No, ma'am. I mean to get some though."

Mary walked to the wagon and crawled in the back. She returned a few minutes later with a thick blanket in her hands.

She walked over to Johnny and held it out to him, smiling.

"This is warm," she said.

Johnny took the blanket. He didn't know what to say to the younger girl. He smiled and nodded, then wrapped the blanket around his shoulders. It was thick and heavy instantly blocking the wind and chill. He wondered if he would ever take it off again.

43

As the wagon moved on during the day Johnny rode next to it on Jack's side and while wrapped in the warm blanket, he was enjoying the trip.

Jack was competent with the reins and the wagon bounced and rolled along easily. One thing was bothering Johnny and had been since meeting the group.

"What's your last names?" he said, looking over at Jack.

Jack looked back at him a moment, then shrugged a shoulder.

"Perkins," he said.

"How far is Lampasas?"

Jack looked over at Johnny again, a look of annoyance on his whiskered face.

"A ways. There are several towns twixt here and yonder though. We will stop at the next one and get some supplies."

"I can't wait to see my cousin, Maddie," Martha said.

She held her balance on the wagon by one hand holding to the seat of the wagon for stability, the other held her bonnet on her head as the wind blew. Johnny looked over at her and then back at Jack. He could hear Mary giggle from inside the wagon bed.

Johnny could only think of the little bit of money he had in his pocket and all the things he needed to stay warm. The blanket he had wrapped around him helped, but a coat would be so much better.

BIRTH OF A GUNMAN

Toward evening, the group rode into a small town. Johnny looked around and was surprised to see it looked like any other town he had been to so far.

A small general store, a few other buildings doing trade, and a saloon. Men and women were milling around the town taking care of what business they had.

Johnny was looking to the general store when a noise from the saloon across the street caught his attention.

Two men were standing at the doorway of the saloon laughing. It seemed they were staring at Johnny.

He felt his anger rising, then he chuckled to himself. He had to look a sight wrapped in a blanket and riding as he was.

Jack stopped the wagon in front of general store. Johnny reined up, unwrapped the blanket from himself, and stepped down. He stretched his legs and stamped them to get the blood moving. He folded the blanket the best he could and laid it inside the wagon bed. Mary smiled at him.

The four entered the general store. Mary went right for the glass jar of hard candy that stood on the counter; she stood staring wide eyed at the contents.

Martha and Jack went to look at the things they wanted or needed while Johnny looked for warm clothes and a coat.

The man came around the counter and walked up to Johnny.

"Need warmer clothes, huh?" he said.

Johnny nodded.

The man picked up a heavy coat that looked like it would be warm enough and handed to Johnny to try on.

"How much is it?"

"I can give it to you for three dollars," the man said.

He looked at Johnny as if he were doing him a favor selling so cheap. It didn't feel cheap to Johnny. He still had a little over four dollars left but he didn't want to spend the majority of his money on a coat.

"I'll give you eight bits for it," Johnny said looking at the man straight on.

The clerk shook his head.

"Listen son, it's three dollars or no coat. Buy it or leave."

The bell above the door jingled and the clerk looked back toward the entrance. Johnny glanced that way. The two men from the saloon entered.

A couple of the customers hastily left as they entered, and Johnny heard the clerk cuss silently as he walked over to the men.

"Can I help you gentleman?" he asked walking up to them.

The two men looked at each other then laughed.

"He called us gentleman, Bob."

The one called Bob laughed harder, the first man looked around the store and said,

"There was a woman came in here. A mighty fine specimen of a woman, too. We came for her."

Johnny looked over toward Jack. Jack glanced at Johnny.

44

The men were dressed in typical rough clothes. They both needed a shave and the smell of alcohol drifted from them as if they wore it as a perfume.

"I want that woman now," he said, stepping forward inside the store.

"Ray, we can always take this little one here. She's young but she'll do, I guess," Bob said as he stroked Mary's hair.

Mary stood stock still, scared to say anything. Tears welling in her eyes.

Jack stepped forward; Johnny did the same.

"You men are asking for a whole lot of problems," Jack said.

There was no stress in his voice. He sounded as if he had just asked for a pound of coffee from the clerk, who was now back behind the counter seemingly scared.

"Is that right? Who are you that I should be afraid of?"

Bob was looking at Mary and grinning. Johnny didn't like it a bit. He decided to speak up.

"Hey, Bob. If you touch that little girl again, I'll kill you where you stand."

Bob looked at Johnny, then laughed again.

"I saw you ride in wrapped in a blanket like an old woman. Hell, you're just a kid. That gun you got tucked in your britches don't bother me," he said.

Johnny never took his eyes off Bob. Instead, ignoring everything the man had said, Johnny said,

"Jack, I'll kill Bob if you will kill Ray."

Jack stepped a little closer to Ray. Now they were only a few feet apart in the little store.

"Martha, you and Mary take cover behind the counter. This won't take long."

Martha gathered Mary to her, the men watching them as she and Mary moved next to the clerk and ducked down behind the counter.

Ray looked at Bob again and laughed.

"This one is unarmed and that one is a kid," Ray said.

"We will take both women once't we kill these two fools." Bob said.

"Jack. If you don't mind, I think I want to kill both of them. Do you mind?"

"I guess not," Jack said, grinning.

The words had not left Jack's mouth and Johnny grabbed his pistol from his waistband.

Johnny brought the pistol up and fired his first shot, hitting Bob in the forehead. The man's head jerked back as a bloody third eye appeared just above his eyebrows.

The gun smoke was thick in the air and the noise was deafening.

The echo had not faded as Ray tried to get his pistol that was in his pocket into action, he was too late. Johnny's second shot hit Ray in the chest. The second bullet hit him in the stomach.

Ray dropped the pistol and slumped to the floor against the counter that Martha, Mary, and now the clerk was hidden behind.

He looked up at Johnny as the younger man walked up to look down on the dying man.

"You're just a kid," Ray said, struggling with the words.

"A kid who killed you. My name is Johnny Cole."

Ray died a moment later. Johnny spat on him.

The clerk raised up from behind the counter as did the other two. He looked over the counter at the dead men then back at Johnny.

"Johnny Cole is your name? I'll remember it for as long as I live. I never seen nothing like that."

He moved to the coat that he had picked out for Johnny and brought it to him.

"Take this," he said, handing the coat to Johnny.

"You all take what you need. It's the least I can do for the fella that killed the Raby brothers."

"I guess the law will be around soon," Jack said.

"No law around now. Used to have a marshal until old man Raby kilt him a few months back," the clerk said.

He looked at Johnny and shook his head.

"You better skedaddle before the old man hears tell of you killin' his boys."

Johnny looked over at the two women then at Jack. He shrugged a shoulder and said,

"I might as well stay the night here in this town. Beats freezing in the cold."

45

Johnny was surprised to find he was treated free of charge not only for the hotel room for himself and the Stewarts but also the evening meal in the lone restaurant.

Folks stared at him and whispered as he walked by which made him feel uneasy and embarrassed a little. He mentioned as much to Jack as they all sat at the table finishing their meal.

"No doubt about it. You are the talk of the town."

"Old man Raby or whatever will hear of what happened then come for the whole lot of us," Martha said, looking around the restaurant that was beginning to fill up with people.

"He won't be after us, Martha. He'll be coming for the ring-tailed tooter that is Johnny Cole," Jack said a little too loud for Johnny's liking.

"I'm not worried about him. He should have raised better sons," Johnny said, sipping coffee.

Martha laughed and looked at Johnny.

"How many men have you killed in your young life?"

"All that needed to be killed, ma'am," he said.

A man walked up to the table. He was dressed in dirty work clothes, a middle-aged man who was starting to bend in his back from the manual labor he endured daily. He ignored the others and looked directly at Johnny.

"Excuse me, I'm the blacksmith in town. I run the livery too. I wanted to tell you, young man, the Raby clan is nothing to sneeze at. They probably done heard of what you did to Ray and Bob. He might be on his way here now."

"You're going to work yourself up in a tizzy, mister if you don't calm down," Jack said.

"Calm down you say. That man and his other two sons are menaces to life on earth. Or at least life in this town."

"Mister," Johnny said. "I'm staying the night. Might stay longer if I want to. Nobody pushes me around. Not for a long time."

"You're just a boy," he said.

"What's your name?" Jack said.

"Kevin."

"Well, Kevin, you don't know this, but this boy is a killer from San Antonio. This is Johnny Cole," Jack said.

People turned to look in their direction. Kevin looked back at Johnny.

"I never heard of you."

"If my friend Jack here keeps saying my name so loudly, he will find out how much of a killer I am," Johnny looked at Jack unflinching.

"No harm meant, Johnny," Jack said.

"If I see the Raby's ride in, I'll let ya know," Kevin said.

He turned and walked away leaving the foursome alone again.

"We should ride out," Martha said.

"Ma'am, y'all go if you want to. I aim to stay here and wait for warmer weather."

"We will head on to Lampasas at first light," Jack said.

Johnny nodded.

"I'll be ready then," he said.

Jack shook his head.

"No, you have work to do here. Raby sounds vengeful, you'll need to face it full on."

"Why? Makes more sense to head on to Lampasas with you."

"You get up there, look us up. I'm grateful for what you did to protect my family."

Johnny said nothing but as Jack stood, he looked down at Johnny.

"Maybe you aren't a bad guy after all. Perhaps there are worse than you that need you to eliminate them."

Jack led his wife and daughter from the restaurant. It seemed all eyes of the other customers were looking Johnny's direction.

He wondered what he would do. He had made his brag to the blacksmith now he had to live with it.

46

As he checked into the only hotel in town, he wanted to know more about the Raby family. He looked at the clerk, who was a soft looking fellow whose brown hair was starting to thin on top. He was watching Johnny sign the register.

Johnny made a scribble of his name and put the pencil down.

He said, "Something the matter?"

The clerk looked up and grinned at Johnny.

"Nope. Things are more right than they have been in a while."

"How so?"

"Bob and Ray Raby were warts on this town. The whole lot of them are. The old man killed the only law we had here. The boys run amok here doing what they want."

"Bob and Ray made a poor decision," Johnny said as he took the room key he was offered.

"That's the Raby's. They are poor decision makers. Maybe they ain't the only ones."

Johnny looked up at the clerk.

"Meaning?"

"They will be coming for you. The old man and his other two boys, Billy and Sam."

"What's the name of this town?" Johnny said.

"It's just called Newtown since it's only been here a year or so."

"So, the Raby's have run wild for a year or so?"

"No. The town come up around 'em. They was here first."

Johnny was tired of hearing of the Raby's. He wanted a room and a decent night's sleep on something softer than the ground.

He headed for the back of the building where the rooms were situated in the one-story building. He found his room and went in, locking the door behind him.

For all of his talk a little precaution might come in handy he thought as he sat his saddlebags and rifle on the bed.

He checked the loads in both guns then looked out the window. The view was the alley behind the hotel. No help.

He laid down on the bed, thinking of what he had gotten himself into. All because he was protecting the womenfolk. Which wasn't even his job, that task was by rights Jack's. But Jack didn't have a gun.

Johnny shook his head to clear his thoughts. He knew the three, the old man and his two sons, would not let the killing go unanswered. They couldn't. Their reputation had to be upheld.

Johnny decided he had nothing to lose. He had already killed enough people. A few more wouldn't matter in the long run. If the Raby's wanted to push the issue, then Johnny would push back.

He was thinking of this as he drifted off to sleep. He was awakened by a noise coming from the front of the hotel. The voices were loud and the main one was talking over the others.

Johnny couldn't hear the words, but he understood the tone. The Raby's had arrived.

Rising from the bed and grabbing his pistol, Johnny looked out the window. It was dark as pitch in the alleyway.

Not one to walk blind into a fight, Johnny wanted to know and see his adversary. He heard the men walking heavily toward his room. With his heart beating faster, and the blood rushing in his ears Johnny made his decision.

He gathered his things, raised the window, and crawled out of the room into the darkness of the alley.

Johnny kneeled on the ground as he heard the door to his room being kicked open. He clung to the shadows and was still, hoping his breathing wouldn't give him away.

He saw a big man walk to the window with a pistol in his hand. He looked out into the alley, then looked right where Johnny was bent down hiding.

The man didn't see him because he looked back into the room and said,

"He done snuck out the winder. You boys find him and string him up."

Johnny counted a slow five, then took off running from the alley to the rear of the hotel.

As he rounded the building, he noticed that the sky was lighting up in the east. Daylight would soon be here. He made his way as quietly as he could to the livery. As he went, he realized he needed another plan.

47

At the livery, he stopped just inside the barn to catch his breath. He looked back toward the hotel to see if the Raby's were in pursuit. A hand touched his shoulder almost causing him to scream.

As Johnny turned to punch the unknown assailant, a voice said,

"It's me, the smithy. They after you, huh?"

Forcing himself to calm down, Johnny took a deep breath. He spoke in a low tone.

"Only until I figure a plan."

"They will come here, so you better have a good one. I won't be kilt protecting a damn fool I tried to warn away."

"I need to store my things except my pistol and rifle."

"Give 'em to me. I'll put it in the office. IF you live you can claim 'em. If not, I keep it all."

Johnny wanted to say something, but he didn't want to take the time. The Raby's were somewhere out there in the fading night.

He gave his saddlebags to the blacksmith then he looked back toward the hotel. The Raby's were coming out onto the porch. The distance wasn't that far, and the old man's voice carried clearly.

"If anyone in town is hiding him, I want them dead too."

The two younger men separated and started in opposite directions looking for Johnny. One of the son's was heading toward the livery.

Johnny waited. Shooting the man would bring his family to the barn on the double and Johnny would be trapped.

BIRTH OF A GUNMAN

He eased into the darkness of the barn feeling for anything he could use as a weapon. His hand fell upon a rolled rope. Johnny picked it up and shook out a loop as quietly as he could.

As he eased to the doorway, he nearly tripped over a horse shoeing pliers. He picked them up in his free hand.

He stood silently waiting for the man to come into the barn. As the man entered into the darkness of the blacksmith shop, Johnny hit him hard on the top of the head with the pliers.

The pliers bent from the force of the blow and the man crumpled to the ground in a heap. Working in total darkness, Johnny worked the loop of the rope over the head of Raby. He pulled it tight around his neck.

Taking the other end, he tried in the darkness to throw the rope over a rafter in the ceiling of the barn. On the second attempt he heard it fall to the ground over the rafter.

Johnny found the end of the rope on the ground. He pulled with all his strength to lift the dead weight of the large Raby brother. He struggled for a few minutes to lift the man.

The man started to wake from being knocked out. He stood groggily on his feet which helped Johnny in his struggle to lift the man.

Johnny gave a hard tug on the rope and felt the man come off the ground, but only a few inches. Johnny wrapped the end of the rope around a support rail on one of the stalls.

The man was kicking and struggling, pulling at the rope as it tightened around his throat.

The Raby brother hung suspended in the air kicking his legs looking for support. He made choking sounds as he lost the battle to breathe. Finally, as daylight was starting to lighten the inside of the barn, the man stopped kicking and fighting and hung limp in the air as the makeshift noose took the life from the man.

The blacksmith came from his office, he looked up at the suspended dead man.

"Well, that is Billy," he said.

Billy's face was dark red, and his tongue was protruding from his mouth.

"It was too good of a way to die for that bastard," the smithy said.

Johnny stood bent over hands on his knees trying to catch his breath. One down, two to go.

48

In his effort to kill Billy, Johnny had lost track of where the other brother and the old man had gone. He needed to be cautious as the sun was now rising and daylight would make being stealthy that much more difficult.

He knew what he needed to do. He needed to saddle up and ride out of town. He also knew he wasn't going to do that.

Johnny Cole knew what he was. A few months shy of fifteen years of age he was a man full grown. He was a little taller than average and would grow more, he had nerve that most grown men didn't possess, and he had a thirst for killing that scared him a little bit.

He had no remorse for any of those he killed. Whether it was the men in Medina, or the Raby brothers. They had all made their choices, and they all died because of them.

Johnny knew he had at least two more men to kill. But he also knew that if the Raby's would ride out and forget about him, he would let them go.

But he knew the two remaining Raby's would not do that. They would make the choice to fight this out. And that choice would lead to more death.

Maybe even his, because Johnny knew that for all his hatred and anger that was in him, he was not immune to dying in the street like a dog either.

As he pulled the pistol from his waistband, he caught movement from the side of the street across from the hotel.

The other brother was moving along the shadows of the buildings, gun in hand, looking forward and behind for any danger.

Johnny had learned one thing in his young life. Only a fool gives a man an even chance when it is live or die.

He also knew that if the Raby's had him in their sights, they would shoot him down without a second thought. Johnny had killed that ranger in San Antonio like that, and he didn't like it. It felt wrong to him.

He stepped from the livery barn looking for old man Raby. Not seeing him, he walked toward the remaining brother as he continued to sneak in the shadows of the buildings.

The morning sun was rising fast, causing those shadows that Raby was lurking in to shrink at a fast pace.

Johnny, his gun low by his leg, walked toward the man, waiting for the Raby boy to notice him.

Like Billy, who was still hanging from the ceiling in the livery barn, Johnny saw that this brother was young, maybe the youngest as he looked a little older than Johnny.

The younger man was scared. Johnny though he could almost hear the man's breathing as he walked toward him.

The man noticed Johnny walking toward him. He froze in surprise to see the man he was looking for in front of him.

Johnny stopped and lifted his pistol, the Raby brother not moving, just staring.

"How old are you?" Johnny said.

"Umm… Nineteen," the man said, caught off guard to be asked such a question.

BIRTH OF A GUNMAN

"You can ride out with your pa and can live to see twenty. If you choose," Johnny took a couple of steps toward the man, his gun still aimed at him.

"Pa won't allow it. He's looking for you hisself over there," he said, nodding toward the alley at the hotel.

"Your brother Billy, he's dead."

"You killed him? And Bob and Ray?" the man said, looking at Johnny in confusion.

"And you too, Sam," Johnny said.

Johnny fired the pistol without hesitation, the bullet hitting Sam in the chest. Sam dropped his pistol in the dirt as he grabbed his chest. He looked down at the gun he had dropped like he forgot he was holding it.

He looked back up at the boy who had shot him. Johnny took a step closer to Sam and shot him again.

This time the bullet hit him in the forehead, jerking his head back. The momentum carried Sam's body back and he fell in the dirt, dead.

Johnny walked up to make sure the man was dead. Bent over and picked up Sam's pistol and stuffed it in his waistband.

Only one more to go.

49

Johnny made a mistake. The two gunshots echoed off the buildings, loud in the quietness of early morning. As Johnny was putting Sam's gun in his waistband, a bullet thudded into the wall of the building, not far from Johnny's head.

The report of the gunshot was loud, and the combination of the bullet hitting the wall and the pistol shot caused Johnny to jump and kneel in the dirt.

There was nothing to protect him from the gunfire, he was in the open, a sitting duck.

Johnny looked over at the hotel alley, which he had ran out of only a half hour before. Old man Raby stood there, pistol in hand taking aim at a kneeling Johnny.

Johnny jumped up and took off running for any cover he could find. A bullet whipped past his head as the sound of the pistol exploded again.

Johnny was able to put the wall of the store he had been in front of between himself and the old man. It occurred to him he needed a better plan.

The old man would not hesitate as Sam had. There would be no surprising him by walking up to him and just shooting him.

Johnny realized he was scared. He laughed a soft laugh. He wondered why he should be scared now. All the killing he had done in the past weeks led to this. He may die as he had lived.

BIRTH OF A GUNMAN

No. Not today and not by someone as unworthy to kill him as old man Raby. Johnny moved to the alley behind the store. He needed to put space between him and his adversary.

He ran down the alley expecting a bullet to hit him in the back at any moment. He made it down the alley and around a building without being killed.

He looked back the way he had come to see if Raby was in pursuit. There was nothing. Johnny moved along the building toward the street, his pistol held in front of him ready to shoot whatever appeared before him.

He made it to the edge of the building. He looked to his right toward the hotel and then across the street to where Sam had died.

He saw Raby kneeling over his son, one knee in the dirt the other knee was supporting his gun hand. He was holding his son's shirt in his free hand.

Johnny was surprised to see that the old man wasn't that old. He was maybe in his early fifties, his hair graying at the sides. He was as big as a house, and it didn't look like fat. His clothes were, like his sons had worn, dirty and worn out.

The old man tilted his head back and yelled.

"You killed my sons. You brought this on yourself young man. I will kill you this morning and send you to hell for what you did here today."

Johnny said nothing. The ferocity in Raby's voice almost made Johnny believe him.

The distance was too far for a chance pistol shot. And, too, Johnny didn't want to give up his position to the man.

He stood where he was and watched the huge man get to his feet. If ever the idea of riding away had any appeal, it was while watching Raby stand up. He was well over six foot tall and big.

Johnny shook his head to clear his thoughts, then eased back into the alley. He needed time to figure out how to confront the elder Raby.

Fighting with hands was out of the question. Getting a surprise drop on him was not going to be easy. Johnny was feeling he was at a crossroads, between a young boy and a grown man.

He certainly had man sized problems with which he had been dealing with for his entire life it seemed.

Johnny took a glance around the corner of the building to see what the old man was doing. It took a moment for what he saw to register. The street was empty.

The elder Raby was nowhere to be seen. Johnny searched the street. The morning sun was bright on the empty streets.

He eased back down the alley from which he had just come, trying to be quiet but feeling as if he made as much noise as a horse stamping the ground.

As he reached the rear of the building, he turned the corner. And ran into old man Raby. For a moment Johnny was shocked to see his adversary standing so close.

The old man hit Johnny.

50

The punch was thrown wide and seemed to Johnny to be in slow motion. He was able to move slightly, the glancing blow still hit with enough impact to knock Johnny down.

The old man yelled something Johnny didn't understand as he had swung at him. Johnny did understand the pistol in the old man's hand coming up and trying to aim.

Johnny had held onto his pistol as he fell, now he brought it up in front of him and snapped a fast shot. Raby's gun spit flame at the same time.

Johnny saw Raby wince and falter a bit. He didn't focus on Raby long. He felt a stabbing pain in his side, knocking the wind from him.

Johnny scrambled to his feet and snapping a quick shot at a still standing Raby he ran down the alley toward the street he had just been looking out on.

He heard Raby fire his gun but didn't know where the bullet went.

Johnny staggered a little as he rounded the building. He was having trouble seeing as his eyes were filled with tears from the pain of the wound in his side.

He dared not look down at it. He had never been wounded before. He had never seen his own blood leaking from his body. Instead of a new feeling of vulnerability, it only made him made at the one who had made him bleed.

He looked over his shoulder to see if Raby was following. There was no one there.

He didn't know where to go. He needed help but knew he couldn't depend on anyone in town to help him. As much as they feared and hated the Raby's, they also had to live here if Johnny was killed. No one wanted to face the potential wrath of old man Raby by giving aid to the man who killed his sons.

Man? That thought hit Johnny hard. He was a man, though not fifteen years old yet. It seemed he had been a man his whole life.

Johnny shook his head and reminded himself to focus. He had a dangerous enemy somewhere around.

He ran to the livery and entered the barn where Billy Raby still hung from the rafter of the ceiling. Johnny glanced at the dead man then stumbled on farther into the barn.

The blacksmith came out of the deeper shadows and stood next to Johnny as he looked out into the street.

"You did it now, huh, boy?" he said glancing at Johnny and the blood on his shirt.

"Yeah, guess so."

Johnny leaned against a support beam and tried to catch his breath.

"Is this town got a doctor?"

"Yep. But first we need to make sure you need the doc or the undertaker. Same fella, different treatment," he spat in the dirt.

Johnny was too tired to say anything.

"Bill Raby will be coming. I won't be here when he does. I'll check in on ya when the shootin' is over."

The man moved silently away from Johnny and disappeared.

BIRTH OF A GUNMAN

Johnny knew he couldn't stay in the barn, though it was nice and cool still in here. He moved to the opening of the barn using the beams and other items as support.

He could feel himself growing weaker as he continued to bleed. This needed to end.

As he made it to the entrance and the double doors of the livery, Raby peeked around the corner. Johnny stopped where he was, still in the deeper shadow of the barn.

Raby came on in the barn, the pistol held to his side. Johnny realized he had seen his dead son.

Raby walked to the hanging man, took a knife from his pocket, and tried cutting the rope.

Raby's back was to Johnny and the man's size prevented him from seeing what he was doing. Billy's body fell to the ground as Raby knelt and held Billy in his hands. Johnny could hear the old man crying.

Johnny felt himself fading, he fought the feeling of passing out. He stepped forward. He took two steps before the noise of his movements made Raby turn around.

Johnny raised the pistol, which suddenly weighed a hundred pounds, toward Raby as the older man turned his head toward the noise Johnny was making.

Johnny shot Raby as he looked at him. The bullet hit him in the forehead causing his head to jerk back. Raby fell upon his son, dead.

Johnny attempted to put his pistol in his waistband, the gun fell to the ground. As Johnny bent to pick it up, the world went dark. Johnny fell in a heap in the dirt.

51

Johnny came awake with a start. The movement caused pain in his side which made him moan a little. He was in a room, on a bed, where and whose he couldn't remember.

He looked around the room. It was bare except for a table along the far wall. There was no window.

Jail. That was Johnny's first thought. He was in jail.

The door opened but instead of a lawman entering, it was a young man who looked happy to see Johnny, which only added to the confusion.

The man, who was in his mid-twenties, looked down at Johnny and nodded.

"Glad you are OK, young man," he said as he checked the bandage on Johnny's side.

"Where am I?"

Johnny laid still as the man did his work.

"You are in Newtown. Do you remember what happened to you?"

Johnny remembered. He had killed an entire family, one by one. Instead of making him feel shame, it made him feel proud. The Raby's needed to die.

Johnny nodded, then said,

"Am I in jail?"

The man laughed, shaking his head.

"No. I am Doctor Elbert; this is my office. I feel if anyone tried to arrest you, they would face a mob."

"How so?"

"You handled a problem the town has faced since its beginning. They, we, owe you a debt of gratitude."

"I don't recall much help from anyone," Johnny said.

"They were scared. Simple as that," Elbert shrugged as if to say that explained everything.

"How long have I been here?"

"Two days. A few more you should be good to go."

Johnny rested a week longer then feeling he had been idle long enough, he got up and got dressed. He found his gun in the drawer of the table in his room. He checked the loads and put it in his waistband.

He walked out of the room into a narrow hallway which he followed to a large room that in other homes would have been the den but was used as an office.

Elbert looked up as Johnny entered the room.

"Ready to ride off, huh?"

Johnny ignored the question, instead he asked one of his own.

"How am I going to pay you? I have no money."

Elbert ignored him. He got up and looked at Johnny, then said, "I'll walk you to the livery. Make sure you get there."

In a few moments they had made it to the livery barn. The man had seen Johnny coming and had his horse saddled and waiting when he got there.

As Johnny checked his saddlebags to make sure his meager possessions were there, Elbert cleared his throat and said,

"You could stay here, Johnny."

"Stay? Johnny said, turning to look at the doctor. "And do what?"

"This town is going to grow, as much as it can with the war coming along. We will need law and order.

You may be too young to be the marshal, but you could be the deputy for whoever we choose to be the law."

Johnny laughed.

"I ain't no law man,"

"I know. You're just a kid basically still. But everyone has to be something when they grow up."

"Guess I have a while then," Johnny said.

"Maybe not. I feel you are already grown. You just ain't older yet."

They were silent for a moment as Johnny adjusted his cinch.

The livery man patted the shoulder of the horse and said,

"Are you signing up for the war?"

Johnny led the horse out of the barn, then stepped gingerly into the saddle. His side still ached a little.

"No," he said. "I have no interest in fighting in that war."

"What will you do then?" Elbert asked.

"Drift until I figure that out. I have some unfinished business back home I need to take care of before too long, maybe."

"You drift very much more, you are gonna get a reputation as a gunman. Then you will be drifting," Elbert said.

"Anytime you drift this way, stop in. We all are in your debt," the livery man said as he stuck his hand out.

Johnny shook the man's hand, then the doctor. He eased his horse forward, testing how the jostling would make his side feel.

BIRTH OF A GUNMAN

As he rode out of town, he looked over toward the little makeshift cemetery that sat at the edge of town. There were five fresh graves in the field. Five more men that had fallen under his gun.

He spurred his horse and rode north. It had been a hell of a few months for Johnny Cole.

Part III

1867

52

Johnny Cole had grown in years and experience since war had come to Texas. His reputation had also grown in proportion to what he had actually done. He had just turned nineteen years old, and he had made for himself a reputation he never wanted.

He had simply wanted to get revenge for his parent's murders and somehow it had spun out of control. He had become a talked about man around campfires and saloons.

The war had raged on, mostly back east, but it hardly mattered in Texas for there was no money, no work, and no honor in what work there was. So, he had taken to riding the rough trails and hanging around the rough places.

He had heard his name mentioned in connection with actions and tasks he had never been involved in or around. But the stories spread. Seemed people liked telling stories of a man, a kid, who would kill at the slightest provocation.

Johnny didn't like it. He hated it actually. But there was nothing he could do about it. Once a rumor starts you play hell stopping it with the truth.

He sat at a table in the saloon and nursed his beer. He looked older than his age, the weather and living conditions made him look to be in his early twenties. No one paid him any attention. There were only a handful of old men in the place at this hour.

The doors swung open, and two men entered. Younger than the few that were in the saloon already. But older than Johnny.

They came in noisily, talking at the top of their voices and laughing with gusto. The men were dirty and unkempt. The stench of unwashed bodies followed the two like a third companion.

They walked to the bar and ordered their beers, then turned and leaned with elbows on the bar top, scanning the room.

The one on the left looked to the other one and started laughing again.

"Them darkies didn't know what hit 'im, did they?"

The other one drank a long pull from his mug, then shook his head.

"That one big one is lucky them women were there. I'd like to kill him deader 'an hell."

"He was a mouthy one."

The bartender stepped closer to them and interrupted their conversation.

"What are you two talking about now?" he said, refilling their glasses.

"Them darkies that settled in on the edge of town last month. We been giving them a welcome."

"Phil, what does that mean?" the bartender asked.

Johnny was listening intently though he appeared to be focused on his own beer.

"What do you think it means?"

Johnny motioned for the bartender, who brought him a fresh beer. Johnny decided to hang around the saloon a little longer, he wanted to find out about the black family. He knew the blacks would not fight for the most part, though some few would as times were changing. He wanted to hear more.

BIRTH OF A GUNMAN

The one called Phil watched the bartender sit the glass in front of Johnny. He then elbowed his friend and looked at the bartender.

"Didn't know you served kids in here."

The bartender glanced back toward Johnny, then looked at Phil,

"Looks old enough to me. I don't want no trouble in here boys."

Phil never took his eyes off Johnny. For his part, Johnny sipped his drink and appeared not to pay any attention to the two men at the bar, though he was aware of Phil looking at him.

After a moment, Johnny stood. He fought down the urge to confront Phil and make a scene. He nodded to the bartender and left the saloon.

53

Johnny stood a moment on the street and looked around the small town. There was not much to look at. This town was much like any other he had drifted into and out of in the past few years.

All the talk seemed to be of the aftereffects of the war or of Comanche attacks out in the western settlements.

He made his way down towards the only restaurant in town. He was hungry and wanted a hot meal.

A man stepped from the alleyway between the saloon and another building. He held a shotgun in his hands, pointed right at Johnny.

Johnny stopped and stared at the man, who was about fifty, with graying hair, and a rough demeanor. Johnny fought to control his temper as he looked at the stranger.

"What's this?" he asked.

"A precaution. That's what it is."

The shotgun never wavered.

Phil, his friend, and the bartender stepped out of the saloon to watch what was happening. Johnny glanced over his shoulder to them, then back at the danger in front of him.

"Against what?"

"Against you Johnny Cole. I heard you was in town."

Johnny lowered his head, at the same time lifted his arms away from his pistol in his waistband.

"You'll have no trouble from me."

BIRTH OF A GUNMAN

"I'm taking you to the marshal's office. I need you to be mindful of this shotgun here as we go."

The man motioned with the barrel for Johnny to walk. Johnny walked the direction indicated. He caught a glimpse of Phil standing in the door of the saloon. There was a sick look to his face.

Once inside the marshal's office, the man had Johnny lay his pistol on the battered and scarred desk then step two steps back.

The lawman sat the shotgun down behind the desk and took Johnny's pistol and placed it in a desk drawer. Only then did he sit down in his chair, motioning for Johnny to sit in the straight back chair on the other side of the desk.

"You aren't going to lock me up?"

"No. Not yet."

They were silent for a moment, then the man rubbed his face with a calloused hand.

"What do you know about our town?"

"Nothing. I'm just passing through."

The man grunted, then stood and walked to the window to look out towards the saloon.

"You saw Phil and his friend Hollis in the saloon. What did you think of them?"

"Didn't give 'em, much thought. What is this about?"

The man turned, making his way back to his chair. His eyes never left Johnny.

"My name is Joe Jordan. I'm the marshal here in town. The law. But only in title, I guess. This place is in turmoil like any other in the state, I guess."

Johnny had no idea what the man was talking about, so he said nothing.

"Anyways, the last thing I need is a trial of some two-bit killer that shouldn't be in Clary anyway. You understand?"

"I do, though I might disagree with the two-bit killer part of your story."

He looked at Johnny for a long moment, then shook his head.

"I can't believe what I'm fixin' to say to you. I know you're a killer. Killed a lot of people from the time you were young, including a lawman or two. Right? Stuff that would have got you hanged if it were normal times. But it wasn't normal times. There was a war brewing, and you did what you had to. I've seen the wanted dodgers on you, heard the stories about you, and figure I know you by reputation."

"OK," Johnny said, not sure where this was leading.

"The point is this. This is a lawless time, and it will get worse. I need help to control what happens in this town."

Jordan stood from his chair and looked at Johnny.

"Have you eaten yet?"

54

Johnny stared up at the standing lawman, shook his head, and said,

"So, what are you saying, Marshal?"

"I need help protecting people in this town. That's what I am saying."

"From what? It looks half dead to me."

"The two you met over at the saloon. Phil and Hollis? They and their friends are a blister on the town of Clary."

"So, pop it. That's what the law is supposed to do, right?"

"I'm trying to pop it, here and now."

Johnny stood and looked at Jordan for a moment.

"By talking to me. That's your plan? You need a better plan."

Jordan reached into his desk and retrieved Johnny's pistol. He laid in on the desk, then looked at Johnny.

"Let's get something to eat and talk this over. If you don't want to help me, ride on out of Clary and never come back."

Johnny looked from the gun laying on the desk back to the lawman.

"I go pretty much where I want."

Johnny had a thought run through his mind for a moment. Kill Jordan and take what he wanted from the town.

He dismissed the idea. He didn't mind killing a lawman now and then, but he was no thief. He only stole what and when he needed to get by through hard times. Which there seemed to be a lot of those times lately.

He picked up the pistol and placed it in his waistband.

"You buy the food and I'll listen to you."

They made their way to the lone restaurant in town. As they crossed the street, Johnny caught a glimpse of the man who was in the bar with Phil, Hollis was that the name Jordan had said? He was standing in the door of the saloon watching them.

Once inside the restaurant, the lone woman brought cups of coffee and Jordan made their order. Beans and bread. As she left, Jordan leaned in a bit and talk to Johnny in a lowered voice.

"I haven't got a better plan as you said earlier. This is the only plan I got, and I thought of it as I seen you ride into town."

Johnny strained to listen as Jordan spoke so quietly.

"OK, let's hear it," Johnny said at normal volume.

"I want Phil and Hollis not to be a problem anymore."

"You want my help arresting them?"

Jordan looked around the room for anyone listening, but they were alone in the restaurant.

"I want them dead."

Johnny sat still for a moment, he leaned in toward Jordan and lowered his voice.

"What?"

"I want them two vultures dead. I don't care how you do it or when. I will back whatever you do and justify it so it's legal. And I'll pay you from the city coffers what I can, maybe forty dollars."

Johnny sat and stared at the lawman, a thousand thoughts running in his mind at once. Johnny sat back in his chair. Of all the scenarios that had ran through his mind when he first encountered the lawman, this was the last one he would have ever thought of. He stared at the marshal, silent.

Finally, he leaned forward and said,

"I have never killed for money before."

Jordan laughed, shaking his head at the same time.

"Please! Don't give me the holier than thou 'I have standards' argument. You saying you never took any money from anyone you have killed? Never?"

"That's different. That was for survival, I needed it, they didn't."

Jordan started to say something, but the woman brought their plates and sat them in front of them. She refilled the coffee cups and moved away.

Neither man said anything else as they ate in silence.

55

Once the meal was finished, they made their way outside walked around the town. Jordan said hello to a few people that were milling around the town as Johnny watched everyone with a wary eye.

He still wasn't sure what Jordan wanted from him, or if this whole thing wasn't a setup to get him to relax while someone put a bullet in his back. He was more cautious the more they walked around town.

"There is a lot not being said. And I'm not sure I trust you. At all," Johnny said.

Jordan looked at Johnny, nodded, and said,

"I been a lawman a long time. Since before Texas was a state. Rode in posse's, killed men who had no regard for the law, and any other thing needed to protect the people of wherever I was. I have never in all my days heard of anyone like you, Johnny."

"Meaning?"

"You been killing people for a long time. Started when you was young and have never looked back. That's the campfire version of your life."

They continued walking in silence for a little bit, then Johnny said,

"I didn't want to. I was kind of forced into the first one. Well, the first three anyways."

"How old are you son?"

BIRTH OF A GUNMAN

Johnny stopped walking and looked dead on at Jordan.

"Don't call me that. Ever," he said.

Jordan noticed the look in Johnny's eyes and something inside him warned him not to push the issue.

"No harm meant. Just the way I speak to young people now and then," Jordan said, as he started walking again.

Johnny fell into step and waked beside Jordan a few feet, then said,

"Nineteen, best I know."

"How many men you killed?"

"I don't know. Eighteen or twenty maybe."

Jordan snorted a short laugh.

"I have been a lawman on the frontier for over thirty years. I'm fifty-two years old and I have only killed three people in my entire life. You say you six or seven times that many."

"Best I can figure. Maybe."

"So, what is two more?"

"I have never hired my gun out. I kill for me or to protect others."

"Others meaning the blacks. I heard of those stories, too. Didn't win you many friends in this day and age, did it?"

"It needed to be done."

"Follow me, come on," Jordan said, picking up the pace of the walk and heading south passed the houses in town.

Johnny walked along in silence as both men said nothing. It unnerved Johnny to talk of killing with a lawman. He cautioned himself not to say anything specific.

185

At the edge of town was a row of what appeared to be hastily built houses that looked as if a strong wind would blow them into the next town.

Johnny and the marshal stopped and watched for a moment.

"The people who live here are the blacks. They have no one to protect them from the foolishness of what's going to happen to them."

Johnny stared at the line of makeshift houses and shelters. To know people lived in these and considered it a good life was disheartening.

"How does Phil and Hollis fit into this?" Johnny said pointing at the scene in front of him.

"Phil and Hollis and others want to run these folks out of town, out of state, out of the country. Take your pick. They make life hard on them all.

They beat and threaten the men, harass the women, and scare the children."

"And you let it happen?"

"No laws against it yet. Heard that Austin is supposed to be working on something but who knows."

Johnny looked at the row of shack houses, then back toward town. The houses in town weren't much better built than the shacks, but it seemed they were colonial mansions by comparison.

Johnny turned around, ignoring the marshal, and walked back toward town.

56

Johnny was sitting in Jordan's chair as the marshal walked through the door. He stopped and looked at Johnny a moment, then walked the rest of the way into the office.

Taking off his hat, he said,

"Didn't expect to see you here."

"I don't like bullies. I never have. So, tell me more of what is happening to the blacks, and how Phil and Hollis fit in it."

Jordan motioned for Johnny to get out of his chair. Jordan then sat down and propped his feet on the battered desk, he looked at Johnny and said,

"Those two and the few like them are the root cause of the problem. They aim to create trouble between those people and the whites."

"I don't hire out my gun. Not to anyone. I've had chances to over the years, but I never took them."

"I can't make you a deputy, that's just foolish talk."

"I had a chance to be a lawman once. In San Antonio."

"What happened?"

"I killed a Ranger," Johnny said, staring at Jordan.

Jordan waived a hand in the air.

"That was a long time ago and different circumstances. But you are a known gunman. You getting on them boys could run them off."

"I don't know. I need to think on it. I want to go over and visit some of the families over there."

Jordan nodded. Johnny left the office without another word.

He walked along the dirty, muddy streets thinking about his life and his deeds. He had a knack for killing. He felt nothing afterwards. He would kill again in the future he knew.

But he had never hired his gun out for money. True, he did take from those he had killed when necessary. Taking for survival was far different than being paid to kill.

He knew he would not do it, would not accept money to kill anyone. But if Jordan pushed the issue, Johnny knew, he would kill him. For free.

He made his way to the houses that made up the black part of the small town. He stood on the street in front of one such house and looked around.

A woman, not much more than a girl, came out onto the porch and stood staring at him openly. It was rare for a black to make eye contact with a white man, much less staring openly at them.

The girl moved off the porch into the dirt patch that passed for the yard of the house. She smiled a little, recognition hit Johnny like a punch in the gut.

"Lula? Is that you?" he said, stepping forward.

"Johnny Cole. Thought you'd be dead by now," she giggled as she came toward him.

There in the open street in front of everyone to see they embraced in a long hug. Lula broke the embrace and stepped back.

"Why you here?" she said.

"Passin' through, mainly. Heard your people were having trouble from some of my kind."

BIRTH OF A GUNMAN

"Them two white men? Yeah, and their friends."

Lula had changed. Not only older in years but in appearance and speech. She looked great to Johnny, who felt an urge when looking upon her that he fought to control. She was a beautiful girl, young lady.

"Last time I saw you or your folks, was San Antonio. The men were talking of war."

"I remember," she said, looking down at the ground. "I remember the river and the dead man."

Johnny was silent.

"Are they around, Tom and Marcus?"

Lula shook her head and looked up at Johnny.

"Pa is dead. Killed during the war. Uncle Joe is all crippled from the war, he drinks mostly nowadays."

"Marcus?"

Lula shrugged her shoulders,

"We sent word to where he last was, up in Kansas somewhere. Maybe he will be coming, maybe not."

Johnny let her words sink in. Tom dead and Joe crippled. The war took a price on everyone it seemed. Lula took his hand, leading him to the porch of their house.

"Ma will be glad to see you, come on in and stay for supper."

The feeling of Lula's hand in his was one of pure delight like Johnny had never known. He would have gone anywhere with her as long as she never let go of his hand.

57

They sat in the tiny, cramped main room of the little house and talked of their younger days. Johnny mainly listened to Lula talk about the past. He had nothing of pride he could really look back upon and speak with longing for.

It occurred to him as he stole glances at Lula's mother that he didn't know her proper name, she had always been Mrs. Sherman to him.

Looking at her now, he saw the changes from what he remembered in his mind. She looked older, though it had only been a few years since he had last saw her. She looked to have aged twenty years.

Her hair was graying, her shoulders seemed stooped as if she carried the weight of the world on them. She seemed tired and resigned to a life without a husband to help her get by.

Looking at her, Johnny said felt sadness for the Sherman's. They had had a hard life that was becoming harder as they aged.

"Where is Marcus, Mrs. Sherman?"

She looked at Johnny and shrugged,

"Heaven knows, son. Kansas, I suspect. We could sure use him here now, though."

"What do you mean?"

"Folks, white folks in this town don't cotton to us niggers bein' here among them. They like to make trouble for us."

"I heard. I think I met a couple of the troublemakers in town earlier. Have they harassed you any?"

"Sure. And Lula. Say awful things to us, threaten us a lot. They killed some too. Though nobody will do anything."

Johnny glanced at Lula; he felt his anger rising. He had always felt she was a nuisance when they were younger, always wanting to hang around him and Marcus. Even though Marcus was older than the two of them. But now, he knew Lula Sherman was more woman than the likes of Phil and Hollis ever had the right to look at, much less bad mouth.

"I will see if I can talk to them," he said, not knowing what else to say.

"Talk? Good luck with that," Sherman said.

Lula smiled at him which made him feel worse for some reason.

"When I say talk, I mean words they will understand, ma'am."

Sherman smiled, nodded her head.

"That's what we want Marcus to do if'n he gets here," she said.

She sat the meal on the table as Lula placed the plates. The beans smelled good, and Johnny realized he was hungry. He ate with gusto.

Only as he was in the middle of his second plate did it occur to him that this might be the only food they had. And they were sharing it with him as he wolfed it down like a starving man. He made a note to bring some supplies to them in the morning.

As they were eating, they heard a horse rein up in front of the small house. Lula looked at her mother and Johnny thought he saw fear in her eyes. But only for a moment.

Lula started to get up from her chair, but Johnny stopped her by placing a hand on her arm.

"I'll see who it is. You eat," he said rising from the table and moving to the door.

A man sat his horse, looking the house over. A black man, Johnny noticed as he sized up the newcomer.

Johnny stepped out on the porch, his hand not far from the gun in his waistband.

"Can I help you?"

The stranger looked at him, then back at the house.

"Your white face is not what I was expecting to find here," the man said, dismounting slowly. "Don't shoot me, now. I have heard stories of Johnny Cole as far away as Dallas."

Recognition hit Johnny then.

"Marcus? About time you show up."

The door opened and Lula and Mrs. Sherman came out onto the porch. Sherman took a moment to realize who it was in her yard, then she bolted from the porch and embraced Marcus in a tight hug followed by Lula. The women were crying.

Marcus was changed as well. Bigger, stronger looking than Johnny remembered. He seemed sure of himself.

Sherman looked back at Johnny. Tears in her eyes and glistening on her cheek.

"It's gonna be all right now. Marcus is here."

58

Leaving Marcus to catch up with his family, Johnny walked back to town. He wanted to gather more information on who was behind the attacks on the blacks in town. He was confident there was more than just the two men, Hollis and Phil and their friends.

He went back to the saloon he had been in earlier, the lone saloon in the little town. As he walked in the bartender gave him a suspicious, but guarded look.

Johnny, despite his young age, had seen such looks before. He ignored the tension he felt from the bartender, walked to the bar with a smile on his face, and ordered a beer.

The bartender silently filled the glass and set it in front of Johnny. The saloon was mostly empty except for two or three men who sat at various tables. None were the two from earlier.

Johnny looked at the barkeeper and sipped his beer.

"When does this place come alive?" he said.

"Alive?" the bartender repeated, "Saturdays mostly, if you call it alive. Times are hard here abouts, if you didn't know."

"You know who I am?"

The bartender nodded,

"I do."

"When I was in earlier there were two fine citizens in here, Phil and Hollis I believe their names are. Where can I find them?"

Johnny sipped his beer and watched the barman's reaction. The barkeeper kept his face neutral as he glanced at Johnny.

"What business you have with them two?"

"My business is mine, sir. What is your name?"

"My name? I'm Charlie."

"How do you feel about what's been happening in this town, as far as the blacks go, I mean."

Charlie said nothing, just looked at him.

"What I mean is, are you okay with them, the black people, being terrorized and their kids being threatened?"

Charlie seemed to slump a little and Johnny saw some of the resistance leave the bar man's face. He looked at Johnny and said,

"No. I don't agree with that at all. I figured you were here to do business with the likes of them two yahoos you asked about."

"Charlie, I want you to do me a favor if you can. The next time either man is in here, mention that I am looking for them."

Charlie smiled, then said,

"OK. I will do that."

"Much obliged."

Johnny left money on the bar top went back out onto the street. The sun was going down, it would be dark soon and he had nowhere to stay the night.

He walked back to the marshal's office, but the doors were locked, and no lights were visible. Having nowhere else to go, he decided to go back to the Sherman's house and see if he could sleep on their porch.

As he walked up to the house, he saw Marcus sitting in a chair on the porch. He was looking back toward town and saw Johnny approaching. Marcus waited until he was at the steps before he spoke to him.

"Lots of things wrong in this town. I hate that my sister and mother are living here. Wish we were back in Medina."

"Where have you been since the war ended?"

Marcus looked at Johnny, shrugged a shoulder. He pulled a tobacco pouch from his pocket and built a cigarette.

"Been driftin'. Doin' what a nigger is allowed to do since we are free."

Johnny stepped up onto the porch and sat in the chair next to Marcus, who offered him his pouch. Johnny declined.

"Been scoutin' for the Army mostly. Was in Kansas when I got Ma's message about trouble in this place. Took me awhile to know where the town was."

Marcus struck a match with his thumbnail and lit the cigarette. He exhaled smoke and said,

"Heard about you even up where I been travelin'. You a killer they say. I believe it, I saw it a time or two. Hope you are ready to kill again. This town has it comin'."

Johnny said nothing, but he couldn't agree more.

59

Early the next morning, Johnny was awake before sunrise. He had slept on the porch after talking with Marcus. Both men decided that the blacks in town had to be protected. They also agreed someone would need to die to make that happen.

Johnny was okay with that. He felt he had died years ago as he watched men murder his mother. He had killed enough men to know life was fleeting and at any moment a bullet could end it.

What he didn't know was who controlled the things that were happening in town. He needed to find Marshal Jordan this morning and gather more information.

During their talk the night before Johnny had not mentioned being offered money to kill the troublemakers. He wanted to keep that part a secret for now as he had not decided if he would accept money or not.

To Johnny's way of thinking, if people had to die, and money was to be made, would it be so wrong to capitalize on that situation.

He pondered this as he folded the lone blanket Mrs. Sherman had given him to sleep with last night. He shook his head to clear his thoughts as he laid the blanket on the chair.

He was hungry. He also didn't want to impose on his friends since they barely had enough to make it on anyway.

As he stepped off the porch, it occurred to him that he had not seen Joe Sherman, Lula's Uncle. Lula had said Joe was injured and spent his days drinking, but Johnny had not seen him or heard the others mention him again.

He stepped off the porch and headed toward town. As he walked, he looked around what he had come to think of as the black part of town.

Shanty houses, shacks, and makeshift shelters made up the houses in this area. A stark contrast to the wooden, painted, and mostly well-kept houses in the other areas of town.

A man stepped from the alley between two houses and looked Johnny in the eye. Johnny started to speak but the man, about forty years old and dressed in clothes that were just shy of being rags, interrupted him.

"You that white friend of the Sherman's?" he said, looking around as if he were afraid someone would hear him.

"Yeah, why?"

Johnny kept his hand near his gun. Even though he had no ill feelings towards the blacks didn't mean they held no ill regards toward him. He knew this and was prepared.

The man noticed Johnny's hand near the gun, laughed, and said,

"You gots no need for that, Mister Johnny. I need you to come get ol' Joe. Take him home."

The man turned and walked back into the alleyway. Johnny hesitated a moment, then followed.

"Ol' Joe? Joe Sherman?" he said as he caught up to the man.

"Ol' drunk Joe more like it. Man ain't took a sober breath in years the way I hear it."

At the back of the alley that separated the houses, a man was laid against the wall of a makeshift dilapidated fence. Johnny had to look twice to recognize the once imposing figure that he knew as Joe Sherman.

Joe was dressed in ripped and torn clothing; he had on boots that had seen better days years ago. His face was covered in white whiskers that made a sharp contrast to his dark face. And he was thoroughly passed out.

The man and Johnny stood looking down at Joe for a moment, then the man said,

"He been here all night, I reckon."

Johnny just grunted a reply.

"I tried getting him home, he just kaput right here."

Johnny remembered the man who had hated him when he was younger. Joe had accused him of leading the white men to their home in Medina when Johnny was just a boy himself. He felt no sympathy for the man.

"Leave 'im here."

Johnny turned and walked away leaving the man standing over the drunk and passed out Joe Sherman.

60

Johnny walked to the Marshal's Office hoping that Jordan was there. He wanted to talk to him about what he had learned since their last meeting.

Jordan looked up from his reading as Johnny walked in. The lawman folded the paper and leaned back in his chair watching Johnny. Johnny took a chipped cup from the shelf above the stove and poured a cup of coffee then sat in the chair opposite Jordan.

"Well, have you made up your mind yet?"

"You definitely have some bad characters in the town."

"I heard one more rode in late yesterday."

Johnny looked at Jordan but said nothing.

"I'm talking about the Sherman boy. He is a ne'er do well if ever I saw one."

"Marcus Sherman is a good man. He scouts for the Army."

Jordan grunted a half laugh, he looked at Johnny. He shook his head as he said,

"You aren't going to take the money for the job are you?"

"I need more information. You know that to end this will take more than getting rid of Hollis and Phil, right?"

"Those are the worst of the lot. Who else are you thinking about?"

"Whoever is behind them, telling them what to do. Giving the orders."

"You don't think those two are capable of scheming on their own?"

"Those two? No, I don't."

"You're young still, and wanted by all kinds of law all over this state. I'm willing to overlook your crimes and misdeeds, but I want something in return. And that something is them two men dead," Jordan stood to his feet as he spoke.

Johnny just looked at him, said nothing. He wanted to get back to the Sherman's house. He wanted to talk to Marcus, but mainly he wanted to see Lula.

That thought struck him momentarily as strange. True, he had known her a long time, since they were youngsters in Medina. She had always been tagging along with him and Marcus even though she and Johnny were the same age.

But to think of her in a way beyond just friendship was strange. Not to mention dangerous, for both, him and her. There were men around who would kill because of such things.

He stepped up on the porch as Marcus was coming out of the house. Marcus looked at him then said,

"I'm going to town. Looking for a man named Phil. Do you know him?"

"I ran into him when I first got to town. I left a message at the saloon that I was looking for him as well."

"Me and Phil about to have a talk about him harassing Lula," Marcus picked up the rifle that was leaning against the wall.

As he stepped around Johnny and off the porch, Johnny said,

"Need company?"

BIRTH OF A GUNMAN

Marcus ignored him and walked on toward town. Johnny went into the house and found Lula and her mother in the small kitchen working over some dough. Lula looked up as Johnny walked in.

"We are making a cake. Hope you like cake."

Standing there in the small kitchen that was hot from the oven, looking at Lula as she worked, Johnny could do nothing but nod his head.

Lula giggled a small laugh as she continued working. Mrs. Sherman seemed to not notice the interaction but she turned to Lula and said,

"I have it from here, you two go out on the porch and talk a spell."

Johnny couldn't remember anyone having a better idea.

61

As they sat on the porch in the chairs, Johnny struggled to come up with anything to say. Lula, luckily, was not lost for words.

"What happens after you leave here?" she asked.

"I don't know," Johnny shrugged his shoulders.

"I asked Marcus that question and got the same answer."

"Lot's of things have happened to make it hard for me to settle in one place I guess."

"So, you're just gonna roam around?"

Johnny didn't answer because he didn't know how to answer. They were silent then for a long moment, then Lula said,

"If you roam this way in the future, I'd sure not mind you stopping for a spell."

Johnny looked at her, smiling.

"Dangerous for you to think that or for me to think what I have been thinking."

Whatever Lula was going to say was lost as a horse and rider rode up to the edge of the dirt that passed for a yard. He had a body draped across the back of his saddle. The rider was a white man Johnny had never seen before. The stranger dumped the body, turned his horse and rode away without a word.

Johnny went to see who the man was that was laid out in the dirt, thinking it was Marcus. As Johnny kneeled to roll the man over, he recognized the clothes from earlier in the morning. Joe Sherman.

BIRTH OF A GUNMAN

He didn't seem to be injured, just drunk. Johnny helped Joe to his feet and tried to walk him to the porch. Joe resisted at first, then seeing he couldn't get loose of the grip Johnny had on him, allowed himself to be led.

Lula was standing on the porch watching, a look of disgust on her face.

"Put him on the sofa in the main room. Lord knows he'll start hollerin' and rantin' soon," she said, opening the door for Johnny.

Once Joe was put to rest on the couch and he and Lula were back on the porch, Johnny was silent for a while.

"What happened to him?" he said, finally.

"A place called Shiloh. He hasn't been right since he got home."

"Your pa, what happened to him?"

"He got kilt in Mississippi at the beginning of the war."

"How did you all end up here?"

"Driftin'. The men left for war and me and ma settled here."

"Lula, I don't know how to say what I want to say to you. But I need you to know…"

She interrupted, "Don't say it. Please. I know already, but you can't be saying things like that."

From the side of the house, Marcus came walking around to the porch. He looked from Johnny to his little sister, a frown on his face.

"Lula, give me and Johnny a moment."

Lula stood and without another word went into the house leaving the two men alone.

"You say you talk to the law in town?"

"Jordan? Yeah, why?"

"I just left 'im. He don't seem to be friendly to our kind."

"He doesn't like you for some reason. I know that."

"Well, whatever the reason is I don't care. He tol' me to deliver you a message."

"What message?"

"Meet him at his office this evening."

Johnny considered that for a moment. Then he looked at Marcus and said,

"You want to come with me?"

62

That evening just before sundown, Johnny and Marcus entered Marshal Jordan's office. The lawman was sitting at his cluttered desk when they entered. He looked up, a frown on his face.

"Didn't know you'd bring company," he said, tossing the paperwork he held aside.

Johnny made no reply, Jordan continued,

"There are folks in town at night that won't cotton to a black man strolling the streets. Even with a white man."

"Are some of those folks the ones who give orders to men like Phil and Hollis?"

"That's what I wanted to talk to you about," Jordan stood and walked to the window. "Those two are at the saloon right now if you want to talk to them. They came riding in a half hour ago."

Johnny looked at Marcus then stepped to the window to stand beside Jordan.

"How much room do I have to talk to them?" Johnny asked.

"Enough, I reckon."

Johnny looked back at Marcus.

"You feel like causing a scene?"

Marcus grinned, nodded his head,

"I am feeling a little thirsty."

The two men left the Marshal's Office and walked across to the saloon. The sun had set and shadows were swallowing last remnants of daylight.

Johnny pushed through the doors of the saloon first with Marcus following. The place was only moderately busy with a handful of men in the place. A couple of dirty men sat at a table by the window and a few more sat scattered throughout the room. At the bar nursing their beer, stood Phil and Hollis.

As Johnny and Marcus walked further into the room, the bartender pointed and raised his voice at them.

"We ain't serving his kind in here. Now he can get out."

Johnny and Marcus stood still as the bartender walked toward their end of the bar. Johnny looked around the room then said to the bartender,

"He's with me. You have a problem with that keep it to yourself. Give us two beers."

The bartender stood still for a moment, looking around at the other men in the place. If he served the two men his friends would look at him with disgust, also if he backed down he would be considered a coward. Johnny knew he had put the bartender in a bad predicament but he didn't care.

Johnny walked to the bar and grabbed two glasses, then walking behind the bar he filled them with beer.

He handed a glass to Marcus as he took a long swallow from his glass. The men in the saloon stared at him open faced and angry.

Johnny could see the anger building in the men's faces at the sight of a black man drinking in their place.

Finally, Hollis pushed himself away from the bar and stared at Johnny, facing him full on.

"This ain't right. You got no right allowing a nigger to drink among respectable people."

Johnny held his glass in his left hand, he set it on the bar top.

BIRTH OF A GUNMAN

"Are you one of those respectable people Hollis? You think it's respectable to harass people because they look different than you?"

"You damn pup…" he started to say.

"Not pup, Hollis. Name is Johnny Cole and I'm the man that's going to kill you. Only decision left to make is whether you die now or later."

The look Johnny fixed on Hollis had the man second guessing his choices. The other men held their silence and stared at the young man making the bold boast. They had heard of Johnny Cole.

"I think it will be later," Johnny said, "unless you push the issue. I want you to deliver a message to whoever gives the orders. I want to meet him."

"Orders?" Phil said, speaking for the first time.

"That's right. I know you two aren't smart enough to plan the attacks on the blacks by yourself. I want to meet the man who runs you."

Johnny drained his glass of beer then tossed the glass to the bartender who caught it. Marcus placed his empty on the bar along with money. They turned and walked out of the saloon.

63

Marcus walked along silent for a moment, then said,

"You sure kick a hornet's nest when you take a notion."

"I'm Ok with that as long as I don't get stung."

In the darkness Johnny couldn't see the expression on his friend's face, but he could hear him make noises deep in his throat as they walked.

"You trust that Marshal?" Marcus asked.

"I don't trust anyone that wears a badge."

As they stepped into the yard, Joe Sherman was coming out of the house onto the porch. Johnny caught a glimpse of him in the light that spilled from the doorway as he stepped outside.

"Joe, where are you heading off to?" Marcus said.

Joe stopped on the porch and although Johnny couldn't see him he seemed to feel the man's stare boring into the two of them.

"That's none of your business, boy."

Joe continued down off the porch. He stopped in between the Marcus and Johnny, who could feel the stare even stronger now.

"I never liked you Johnny Cole. You been nothin' but trouble for my family since you come around when you was a kid."

Joe walked away without another word.

Johnny stood there imagining he could see him walk off toward town.

He turned to Marcus and said,

"What happened to his wife?"

BIRTH OF A GUNMAN

Marcus walked toward the porch, Johnny followed.

"Dunno. Ma said she just up and left one day, not saying nothing to no one. Joe was away at the time."

As they entered the house, the stifling heat was enough to make Johnny want to turn around and go back outside. But before he could Lula stood from her chair in the living area greeted them both, looking at Johnny a little longer than she should have.

He felt himself flush and hoped Marcus didn't notice.

"Unc went to town," Lula said as she led them to the kitchen for dinner.

As they sat at the table Lula served up some beans and poured coffee for them. The men ate in silence which seemed to irritate Lula who cleared her throat a few times as if she wanted to speak, and then changed her mind. Finally, Marcus looked at her and said,

"Say what's on your mind."

Lula looked at both men for a moment, then said,

"I hate it here. I want to go away, somewhere else."

"This does seem to be a bad place for our kind. But it's bad in places as of yet."

"Maybe that will change in a few years," Johnny said.

Marcus snorted a laugh.

"Not likely."

"Well, either way I'm not staying here. I can't."

They finished their supper in silence. Johnny took his leave and went outside to sleep on the porch.

In few minutes Lula came outside to talk to him. He felt uncomfortable with her alone out on the porch in the dark. She seemed unconcerned.

"I meant what I said in there. I want to leave."

Johnny tossed his blanket on the porch and toed it out straight with his boot.

"Where do you think you can go?" he asked as he worked.

"With you."

Johnny looked at her.

"Me? What?"

"I think I love you, Johnny. I know I care for you and I know you feel something for me. We can run away together."

Despite his best effort Johnny laughed.

"I'm an outlaw. I have a price on me. The only reason I ain't in jail now is because Marshal Jordan hasn't locked me up. You know my bloody past."

Lula stepped forward, closer to Johnny. He could feel the heat of her body and smell the sweat of her skin.

"You're being foolish, thinking such things."

"I know your past. Just think about it."

"There is not…"

She kissed him cutting off whatever he was going to say. The kiss was long and felt good. He didn't want to stop. She stepped back and without another word went into the house.

Johnny lay down on his blanket but had trouble sleeping. He kept thinking of that kiss. That warm wonderful kiss.

When sleep came he dreamt of kisses, and at one point he thought he heard fireworks.

64

Johnny was awakened by someone nudging his ribs with a boot. It started lightly and Johnny ignored it. They became harder and when he realized he wasn't dreaming, he opened his eyes to Marshal Jordan standing over him.

"You and your friend probably need to come with me. Now."

Johnny got up, stuffed his gun in his waistband, grabbed his hat, and rolled the blanket. He went inside and returned a few minutes later with Marcus.

Daylight was just breaking and Marcus rubbed his eyes and stared at the lawman a moment, then said,

"What is wrong now?"

"You two follow me."

Jordan led the way toward town. Johnny figured they were heading to the Marshal's Office but as Jordan kept walking past the office Johnny grew confused.

Jordan led the way down an alley beside the saloon.

"Is Joe Sherman drunk again?" Johnny said.

They rounded the corner of the saloon and Jordan stopped.

The morning sun was beginning to chase the shadows away, and it promised to be a hot day.

Lying on the ground leaned against the back wall of the saloon was Joe Sherman.

He wasn't dead drunk. He was just dead. His throat had been cut, the front of his dirty shirt covered with blood. From the look of his face someone had beaten him before killing him.

Marcus stood staring down at his uncle. Johnny wanted to turn away but he couldn't.

"They beat him and cut his throat," Marcus said.

Jordan nodded.

"And shot him, too."

"Who?" Johnny asked.

"Don't know. I can guess though. You and Marcus riled them up yesterday."

"Those two white men from the saloon?" Marcus said turning his back to his dead uncle's body.

"Phil and Hollis," Johnny said turning and walking out of the alley.

Johnny left Marcus and Jordan to handle things with Joe. Johnny felt he had other things to do.

As Johnny stood on the street gathering his thoughts, Marcus was suddenly beside him.

"You ain't doin' nothing without me."

"I need my guns."

Johnny walked toward the Sherman house again with Marcus following. Along the way Johnny could feel his anger rising, to the boiling over point.

He thought about what brought him here to this point. He had been passing through town on his way to somewhere else when he was confronted by a Marshal Jordan and offered a job to kill the local bullies.

BIRTH OF A GUNMAN

If Jordan had been so inclined, Jordan could have locked him in jail for any number of crimes through the years. Instead, Jordan had turned a blind eye. Why?

Maybe the town did have problems Jordan couldn't solve on his own, or maybe it was a way to eliminate Jordan's enemies without the marshal getting involved.

When they entered the house, Lula and her mother were sitting at the small table in the kitchen. Mrs. Sherman stood as Johnny and Marcus entered the room.

Marcus explained what had happened to Joe. As Marcus told the story, Johnny went to his gear stored in the corner of the front room. Fishing in his bags, he retrieved his extra pistol, and then took the shotgun from the blanket it was wrapped in.

Marcus came into the room and watched.

"He was our uncle. You don't need to get involved."

"Involved? I have been involved since I got to town. Joe was killed because we strutted our stuff in the saloon last night," Johnny said checking the loads in his guns.

"I know that. Joe didn't even like you, though."

Johnny looked at Marcus and shook his head.

"Like has nothing to do with this?"

As Johnny stepped out of the house, Jordan was standing in the front yard waiting. The lawman stared at Johnny a moment, then said,

"Our deal still holds. Hollis and Phil."

"I want the man who tells them what to do."

Johnny pushed past Jordan and walked back toward town.

65

The morning sun was burning hot as Johnny made his way toward town. Jordan was walking beside him keeping his silence. When they reached the street in front of the saloon, Jordan cleared his throat and spat in the dirt.

"The man you want owns the saloon."

"The bartender?"

"No, not the bartender."

Jordan pulled a small pocket watch from his shirt pocket, checked the time, then dropped it back in his pocket.

"He will be bringing his deposit to the bank in a few minutes. Hollis or Phil will be with him."

"Why do you want those two dead so badly. You bound to have had chances to lock them up, why ask me to kill 'em."

"Those two are protected by their boss. Nothing happens in town without permission from Mitchell, including my job."

"So, self preservation holds you back from your supposed duty?"

Jordan remained silent.

The men came walking from the other end of town that led to the residential area, the man in the middle was older and dressed better than the two on either side.

Johnny recognized Hollis and Phil right away. There was something vaguely familiar about the man in the middle. Something Johnny couldn't put his finger on.

BIRTH OF A GUNMAN

The men were too far down the street to get a close look at. Johnny glanced at Jordan.

"That the boss?"

"That's him."

Johnny took two steps out to the street intending to cut them men off. A gunshot broke the silence of the morning air, echoing off the buildings in town.

A brief moment Johnny thought the men were shooting at him and Jordan, but then Hollis went down in a heap.

Shouts of surprise came from the two men walking with Hollis. Phil drew his pistol from his holster and looked around.

A shot kicked up dirt from between the two men, as the boss man cursed and Phil returned fire blindly in the direction of the shot.

The boss ran in a crouched stance toward the saloon. Phil kept an eye on their back trail as he followed his boss.

Neither man seemed to notice Johnny or Jordan standing in front of the Marshal's Office as they made their retreat. Johnny caught a glimpse of the boss as he turned to shout something to Phil.

Johnny felt his anger rise as he caught a glimpse of the man. He grabbed Jordan by the arm forcing him off the street back into the office. As he slammed the door shut, Jordan jerked his arm free.

"What's got into you?"

"The boss. Tell me about him."

"Why now?" Jordan said moving to the window to look out.

"I know that man, from Medina, a long time ago."

"You can reminisce later; right now your black friend just started a fight and left the meanest one alive."

"Meaning?"

"Hollis was the follower of the group. Phil is the rattlesnake, then there is Mitchell."

Jordan was still looking out into the street from the window; he stepped back a little bit and looked at Johnny.

"Open that door, here comes the Sherman boy."

Johnny opened the door and a moment later Sherman came running in, out of breath, Johnny closed the door.

Sherman straightened trying to catch his breath, an old Hawkin rifle held in his hands.

"I got one of them," he said.

"Yeah, you did. The weakest one, now the two lions are in the saloon together. And I am caught in here with you two," Jordan said, focused on staring at the saloon.

"Is there a back door?" Johnny said.

Jordan jerked his head toward the lone cell to a tiny walkway to the left of the cage. Johnny and Marcus followed the walkway to a door that opened out to the back of the building.

They left Jordan standing at the window, staring at the saloon.

66

At the rear of the building, Johnny led the way to an alley that separated the Marshal's Office from whatever building was beside it, Johnny couldn't remember, nor at the moment did he care.

At the mouth of the alley where he had a view of the saloon, he cast a quick glance across the street toward where the men were holed up.

He leaned back against the wall taking cover. He looked at Marcus.

"The leader, the one responsible for all this mess between the blacks and whites, is Mitchell Goodson. You know him?"

"I never heard of him."

Johnny exchanged his shotgun for the rifle Marcus held. Marcus made the exchange silently, checked the loads on the shotgun, then said,

"Who is he?"

"The man who took me in when for a moment when my folks were killed. I found out later he was part of the group that killed my pa."

"There seems to be too much killing going on," Marcus said.

"Just a couple of more, then I'll be content."

Johnny checked the load on the rifle, he sighted it in on the saloon window. He pulled the trigger, the explosion loud in the quiet street. The window blew into a thousand pieces as a yell came from the saloon.

Johnny handed the rifle back to Marcus and took his shotgun back.

"There is a backdoor to the saloon. I'm going to circle around to it. You watch this saloon, anyone sticks their head out, take it off," he said.

Marcus nodded as he reloaded the rifle. Johnny took off back the way they had just come from, wanting to get to the saloon before Phil and Goodson could escape.

Johnny worked his way behind the buildings until he found a way to cross the street that would be unseen from the saloon.

He stood at the far end of town between the livery and the Marshal's Office staring into the empty street. Once the shooting started what people were out and about took shelter. As he was forming a plan, he heard someone from the saloon shout into the now empty street.

"Jordan, you better get hold of that boy and see to it he hangs for shooting a good man down."

There was silence from Jordan's office.

A shot rang out, the bullet hitting the doorjamb of the saloon, splinters flying in the air. At the same time, Marcus ran across the street toward the alley beside the saloon.

A pistol shot rang and echoed, and Marcus fell to the ground in a heap. Dirt flying as his momentum hit the ground. He laid still.

Johnny ran across the dirt street from where he was. A bullet kicked up dirt behind him as he made it to the other side of the street.

He made it to the rear of the buildings that led behind the saloon. The same area they had found Joe Sherman dead a few hours before.

BIRTH OF A GUNMAN

As Johnny slowly walked, checking his surroundings, the back door of the saloon opened. Johnny ducked behind some empty barrels and watched the door. It was Phil, pistol in hand coming from the saloon, alone.

Phil looked one way then the other, then came out of the saloon and closed the door gently. He eased toward the alley away from where Johnny was crouched.

From around the corner, on the street side of the alley, Marcus Sherman stumbled around the building and collided with Phil.

The impact knocked Marcus down and caused Phil to stumble back. Marcus lay in the dirt staring up at Phil, helpless.

"You're tough to kill, ain't ya boy?" Phil said, raising his pistol.

Johnny took careful aim with his own pistol and shot Phil. The bullet hit him high in the back shoulder, spinning him around. As Phil spun around, he was raising his pistol to shoot, but Johnny shot him again. The bullet hit him in the forehead near the left eye, a red mist flew from Phil's head and he fell dead beside where Marcus still lay.

Johnny walked over to Phil to make sure he was dead, then checked on Marcus. He leaned down and looked at the wound to Marcus's side.

"Thought I told you to wait."

"I don't work for you," Marcus said, struggling to catch his breath.

"I'd probably fire you if you did," Johnny said as he tore Marcus's shirt to press to the wound.

"Hold this, I will be back."

Johnny stood and walked to the back door of the saloon.

219

RONNIE ASHMORE

67

Johnny gingerly touched the door handle, the door was unlocked. He reloaded his pistol, then took another look at the injured Marcus and the dead Phil. He shook his head in wonder.

He eased the door open slowly, quietly. He stepped into doorway which opened on a type of storeroom. He eased the door closed behind him and stood letting his eyes adjust to the gloom of the darker room.

From upfront in the main saloon area, Mitchell yelled again.

"Jordan, You better do as I say, once Phil handles these two troublemakers, you'll have hell to pay."

While Goodson was talking Johnny used the noise to move into main saloon. Goodson stood at an opened window looking out.

For a brief moment Johnny wondered why Jordan wasn't doing anything. Then it occurred to him. Jordan was waiting to see who came out a winner in this ordeal. If Johnny were successful then Jordan would attempt to arrest Johnny. An instant reputation would be made of being the man who captured the notorious outlaw Johnny Cole.

Ahead and to his left, stood the man who had tried to take him in when his parents were murdered. A man, whom he later discovered, albeit through rumor, had a hand in the death of his father. A man he had wanted to kill since that first day of killing in Medina so many years ago.

Johnny stepped into the saloon, scarping a boot on the hardwood floor.

Goodson laughed, and said as he turned,

"Phil, my boy, did you kill both…"

His sentence was never completed as he stared into the face of Johnny Cole, his pistol pointed at him.

"Let's you and I have a talk, Goodson. Tell me how my father's death was a terrible thing. You know like you did when I was a child."

Goodson looked over Johnny's shoulder, and then back at Johnny.

"Where's Phil?"

"Dead."

Johnny motioned with the barrel of his pistol and Goodson walked slowly toward it his hands held wide from his sides though he was unarmed, he pulled a chair back and sat.

"How did you end up here?" Johnny asked as he moved over behind the bar and poured himself a shot of whiskey.

Johnny never drank much, but he hoped the liquor would settle his nerves. Goodson watched him for a moment in silence, then sighed, and said,

"Martha died. There was nothing left for me in Medina as word got around what happened with your folks. We were pretty much shunned. We moved on, she died on the trail."

"She was a cold woman," Johnny said, pouring another shot of whiskey.

"She took you in when you were alone."

BIRTH OF A GUNMAN

"I was alone because you and your friends killed my parents. My mother was raped and shot in the head. But you knew that. That was why you happened to come by our place that day."

Johnny tossed his whiskey back, poured one more shot, grabbed a second glass, and poured a second shot.

Johnny could feel his eyes burning. He told himself it was the whiskey but he knew better. He had made himself a promise, years ago, standing over the unmarked grave of his parent's not to cry ever again. He had held true to that promise, even after all the things he had done, and people he had killed.

As he moved from behind the bar, the two glasses held in his left hand, he said to Goodson,

"I thought a long time of killin' you."

Johnny handed Goodson one of the glasses, he took it with a hand that trembled slightly.

"I'm unarmed."

"I've been shot before. I take a dim view of it. It works out better for me if you are unarmed."

Johnny downed his shot of whiskey. Goodson watched, then, his hand shaking visibly now, attempted to drink his down.

Instead, Goodson fumbled with the glass spilling whiskey then dropped the glass to the floor. At the same time he reached his right hand under his coat and attempted to stand.

Johnny shot him. The bullet hitting him in the chest, knocking him to the floor, his gun went skidding across the wood floor out of reach.

Johnny walked up to Goodson, who was struggling to catch his breath and aimed his pistol at him.

"Your friends are in hell waiting on you," Johnny said, then pulled the trigger.

68

Johnny walked back to the rear of the saloon to check on Marcus. His friend was alive, but in a lot of pain. Johnny carefully lifted him to his feet and they walked down the alley toward the street.

Jordan met them at the mouth of the alley. He looked from one to the other, then said,

"Is it over?"

Johnny ignored the question.

"We need a doctor."

Seeing the Marshal on the street inspired the citizens who had taken cover to appear out of nowhere on the street as well. In no time a young man appeared saying he was the doctor and took charge of Marcus.

Johnny was left standing alone in the street looking around at the people. Cowards. That was Johnny's first thought. There were no doubt some good people in the crowd but they had been bullied into inaction by a bunch men who hated based only on skin tone. And the so called good people did nothing as the blacks, men, women, and children, were beaten, degraded, and victimized. It was a fitting word, cowards.

Later that evening, Johnny was gathering his things from the Sherman house in preparation of leaving when Lula came walking into the yard. She stepped up onto the porch and looked at Johnny.

"Marcus will be all right. Does this mean you ain't stayin'?"

"No. I can't."

"I wish you would. I think I love you," she said, staring at him full on.

Johnny stopped rolling his blanket and looked at her. She was a pretty woman, and she would make a fine wife to someone, but not him.

"I think I love you too, Lula. But I can't put you in danger. I'm a hunted man. I killed a lot of people."

"People like Goodson?"

"People like Goodson seem to be everywhere, in charge of everything. I have to keep moving."

Johnny picked up his blanket roll, and put his shotgun under his left arm. He stepped toward Lula, stopped in front of her. He wanted to kiss her, but that would be too brazen of a thing to do on the porch in front of everyone.

He was saved from making a choice by the sound of a horse approaching. He looked out to the street, he saw Jordan reining up with his saddled horse on a lead rope.

Johnny stepped off the porch, Lula following.

"Is that my horse?" Johnny asked.

"Figured you'd want to get started to wherever you're going."

Jordan dismounted, then pulled a cloth sack that jingled from the inside pocket of his shirt.

"I owe you money, as promised."

"Whatever is in that pouch, give it to Lula. They need it more than I do. Besides, they're the ones that suffered from Goodson and them."

Jordan tossed the bag lightly in his hand, then handed it to Lula who took it silently, staring at Johnny.

BIRTH OF A GUNMAN

"You killin' Goodson, that was personal, weren't it?" Jordan asked.

"I killed a lot of people in my young life. It's always personal."

Johnny tied his gear to the rear of his saddle as Jordan released the lead rope from around the horse's neck.

"They will hound you until they run you to ground, you know that, right? Hell, you're still a young kid but you already have a reputation as a gunman. You're known as a dangerous man."

Johnny stepped into the leather, settled into the seat, and then placed his folded hands one over the other on the saddle horn. He looked at Lula for a long moment, wondering briefly what it would be like to stay with her. He then looked at Jordan.

"Marshal, I have an interest in this town. I expect I'll be coming around now and again to check on those interests. I'll expect you to give me a wide berth when I am in town."

"Well, I am a lawman, after all."

"Your law protects people like Goodson and his kind while turning your backs on folks like them," Johnny nodded toward Lula. "I have no respect for your law. If any harm comes to this family or their people, I'll come back and show you what a young gunman can do."

Johnny tipped his hat to Lula, something no white man had ever done to her, and then spurred his horse out of town.

It felt good to be on his way to somewhere else.

More Books by Ronnie Ashmore

Colby PD Series
Family Secrets
Colby Nights

John Riley Bounty Hunter Series
The Losing Trail
The Killing Trail
The Vengeance Trail
The Deceiving Trail
A Bullet for Malo
The Claren Range Dispute

Sam Bolton Ex Ranger
Duty Bound
Fighting Men
Crooked Trail

Other Books
Last Stand for a Bad Man

Non-Fiction
Lessons on Leadership:
Leading Behind the Badge

ABOUT THE AUTHOR

Ronnie Ashmore is the author of several short stories and novels focusing on crime fiction and westerns.

When he is not working or writing and has some spare time, he enjoys playing golf, fishing, and traveling.

You can email him at ronnieashmorebooks@gmail.com

THANK YOU FOR READING!

If you enjoyed this book, we would appreciate your customer review on your book seller's website or on Goodreads.

Also, we would like for you to know that you can find more great books like this one at www.CreativeTexts.com